With Best Wishes

Beverly Martin

THE
SPELL SINGER
and other stories

THE
SPELL SINGER
and other stories

**In association with the
National Library for the Handicapped Child**

Foreword by Jack Ashley MP

Consultant Editor
Beverley Mathias

*Illustrated by
Mairi Hedderwick*

Blackie

© Nederlands Bibliotheek en Lektuur Centrum.
Used with the permission of the
National Library for the Handicapped Child.

First published 1989 by Blackie and Son Ltd

British Library Cataloguing in Publication Data.
The spell singer and other stories
    1. Children's short stories in English,
    1945-/ Anthologies
    I. Mathias, Beverley
    823'.01'089282 [J]

    ISBN 0-216-92737-4

Acknowledgements

The Publishers would like to thank the following for their kind
permission to reprint copyright material in this book:

Heinemann Young Books Ltd for 'Gone to Sea' from *The White
Horse Of Zennor* by Michael Morpurgo, originally published 1982
by Kaye and Ward Ltd, copyright © 1982 Michael Morpurgo;
Curtis Brown (Aust) Pty Ltd for the extract from *I Can Jump
Puddles* by Alan Marshall, copyright © 1955 Alan Marshall.

Blackie and Son Ltd
7 Leicester Place
London WC2H 7BP

Printed and bound in Great Britain by
Courier International Ltd, Tiptree, Essex

Contents

Foreword

In any discussion of disability, one of the most common expressions is 'the disabled'. This implies a non-existent homogeneity and obscures the individuality of disabled people.

These vivid, moving stories show disabled children as individuals. They reveal their sensitivity, resilience, frailty and courage. The children are not stereotypes but lively human beings. Their stories will give immense pleasure to many people, adults and children, disabled and non disabled. I warmly recommend them.

The Rt Hon Jack Ashley CH MP

Introduction

Nearly all children at some point read a book about which they can say 'that's me!' Children who have a disability or handicap find it difficult to discover 'me' in many of the children's fiction books they read. So often we forget that these are ordinary children doing the same things as everyone else, sometimes with more difficulty, sometimes not. In this collection of short stories about a number of enterprising, adventurous and lively children, there are numerous 'me's', and all of them have some form of disability or handicap. One goes to witch school, another foils a handbag snatch, one helps solve a bank robbery, another teaches through love, and in one story the heroine is a girl who has never spoken. All of the stories have been written by established children's writers, and the drawings by Mairi Hedderwick bring the children to life.

Beverley Mathias
Director, NLHC

The Spell Singer

ANNA LEWINS

'I can't read it.' Katy winced up at the faces — embarrassed, pitying, bored faces. 'I'm sorry, Mrs Batsleer. I can't make the words keep still. If the Spell goes wrong . . .' She shuddered. 'I don't know what might happen.'

Fifty girls sighed together and Mrs Batsleer sank deeper into her chair. Behind her, the school motto glittered in gold on old stone . . . 'Our magic can move the stars.'

'Katherine, please try. One word at a time, like Miss Henbane showed you.' She smiled encouragement. 'Follow your finger, remember. Please try, Katherine. I want everyone to have a chance at this. We'll all duck and you read what you think it says. I'll worry about the Spell going wrong.'

The fifty girls stopped sighing and began to shuffle in the direction of the hall doors. A Batsleer frown stopped them. When Mrs Batsleer frowned and stretched her bats' wings behind her, no one dared move. She could fly faster than any broom in the school.

No way out, then. Katy licked her lips, dragged her finger along the giggling mess of letters and started to read the Dragon Spell. 'I call thee now. Come . . . Come . . .' So far, so easy. 'Dragon. Come give thy fire . . .' It had to say that, anyway. That

11

was what they wanted. Now the Spell Words. 'Hinn ketyr monti . . . monti . . . Pesto?'

The wrong words. The wrong Spell! Mrs Batsleer yelped as blackbirds clattered out of the trophy cupboard. 'Close the hall doors! Don't let them out! Canta bellos!'

Blackbirds swooped under the high, hall roof, darting between the wooden beams.

'Canta bellos!'

Flapping, feathers falling . . . And a metal echo when the second Spell caught them from behind. A hail of silver cups bounced on the hall floor, black wings twitching back to curved handles. The potion trophy was luckier. It escaped, a blackbird with a silver beak swinging over the bicycle shed to freedom.

Katy's finger ached and glued itself to the paper but she had to go on. 'Fire the gift. Fire the luck. Donna eti . . . eti . . .' She blinked and looked into Mrs Batsleer's eyes. 'Flump?'

'Oh no!' Mrs Batsleer leapt up in a jumble of wing and long skirts. Girls screamed as their headmistress's chair groaned into a dinosaur. Small head, big eyes, neck like a python and a tail that reached to the far side of the hall. The dinosaur lumbered backwards and its roar of alarm rattled the windows.

'Don't panic, girls! He won't hurt us.' She hovered above its long neck. 'I hope . . . Katherine, dear, I think you'd better stop. We can't really afford to lose any more furniture . . . Go back to your place.' She managed a hollow smile. 'You

tried very hard.'

Somehow, Katy forced a shaky nod but her lips could not smile. At the side of the hall, several girls rolled their eyes scornfully, and she made herself look at them until they stopped. Other girls picked themselves up, white with shock. She had really frightened them, this time. Head down, she slid into the front line and hoped that none of her friends tried to cheer her up. That always made it worse.

Mrs Batsleer and the dinosaur studied each other. As dinosaurs go, it seemed quite harmless. Bits of chewed grass hung from its mouth so Mrs Batsleer decided that it was vegetarian and settled on its warm back.

13

'Now, has everyone read the Spell? I haven't missed anyone? Good.' She patted the dinosaur's neck. 'In that case, Assembly dismissed. We'll meet here at three this afternoon and go to the dragon's cave together. I don't have to tell you, girls, how important it is that one of you calls the dragon.'

She did not say, 'If none of you can, the school closes. The town's luck leaks away. Something terrible happens.' But everyone knew what she meant. Her glossy wings folded too flat and they only did that when she was very, very worried.

Whispering and pulling faces, the girls trooped into the corridor. Katy followed too fast and slid to a halt, Janice Parker's long back right in front of her face.

'Honestly, she's a real dumbo,' Janice sniggered, remembering the blackbirds. 'I don't know why Batty lets her stay here. I mean, if she can't spell words, how's she going to Spell magic? One of these days she's going to do something really stupid. That dinosaur might have been a meat-eater. We might have been its next meal.'

Janice's three friends gulped embarrassment, glancing at Katy and away. They coughed and twitched their noses at Janice to stop her but Janice didn't take any notice. She never took notice of anyone.

'And Louise says Dumbo's dad's always behind on her school bills. If I was Batty, I'd throw her out.'

With no space to walk around Janice's big feet,

Katy had no choice. She touched the girl's shoulder.

'Excuse me, Janice.'

Janice's mouth fell open and Katy smiled and squeezed past her. When she had turned the corner and was out of sight, she put her head down and ran.

It wasn't fair. She *could* read, maybe not easily, but Miss Henbane's lessons had helped her to put letters into words. Now letters played their games with her but she was ready for them and fought back. A 'b' might try to look like a 'd' and double letters wriggled from side to side and pretended to be triples. Or the same word made a different shape every time she squinted down at the paper. And then she sometimes saw the words well enough but said them back to front, anyway. She had called Mary Helen, 'Hairy Melon.' Oh yes, Katy could read but when the whole class watched, she could not stop the letters dancing and everyone waited for her to be stupid and turn the floor into treacle. Being dyslexic was hard enough. Being a dyslexic witch was horrible.

Mr Meers heard her run around the gravel path to the herb garden and his flock of starlings stopped weeding to watch. The crows re-planting the lettuces croaked a hello.

Maybe she had wanted to come here. Katy was not sure, but she was suddenly glad to see Mr Meers and his birds.

'Hello, crows.' She rubbed her nose, hard, and grinned at Mr Meers' hat.

15

A pair of sparrows had nested in Mr Meers' hat for as long as anyone could remember. Bits of twig and white globs of droppings smothered the old felt. The baby sparrows had just started to fly. One missed and landed on Mr Meers' nose. Its sharp claws dug into his nostrils and his eyes watered, but he did not mind.

'Mr Meers—' Katy fought to get her breath back. 'Did you hear what I did?'

'Everyone heard. Like a brass band in a jam jar.' He shook his head, careful not to upset the baby bird. 'Dinosaurs! It'll be terry . . . terrydactyl-thingies next. You're dead risky to have around.'

'I know.' Katy's grin crumpled. 'But I've got to keep trying, even if they say I'm stupid.' She shuddered and dug her chin into her chest so that he wouldn't notice. 'I'm not stupid. I know I'm not. If I could remember them, I wouldn't have to read them.'

'Ah!' Mr Meers turned to his starlings and they gave him a knowing look. 'Remember, is it? And what about that rule-thingy? About how many words it's safe to remember? If you're after Spelling up a dragon, you'd better not say the wrong thing.'

'I wish that tourist hadn't sneezed.' Katy bit her lip. 'Stupid man. Why couldn't he put his hand in front of his mouth? He sneezed the flame right out. It'd been there for years and years . . .'

Mr Meers humphed a laugh. 'And a sneeze blows it out!'

Everyone knew the old story. A hundred years

16

ago, the town had had a run of bad luck, trees falling through roofs, floods in summer, plagues of monster insects. They had blamed the witch school for letting unluck escape from a Spell lesson. After a terrible Council meeting, when some people had wanted to tear the school down, the Mayor had ordered the school to put the town's luck back or leave. None of the teachers had known what to do and they had got ready to evacuate the school. Then, one of the youngest girls had had an idea. A brave, dangerous idea. She had crawled into the cave on the hill and asked the cave dragon for some of its fire. To everyone's amazement, the dragon had not eaten her. It had given her fire and she had carried it in her sock to the town hall.

As long as the green flame burned, the town let the school stay on, rent-free, and enjoyed good luck. Now the flame was dead. If it was not burning again in a day and a night, the people would close the school and the girls would have to go home half-taught. That meant that they would never be allowed to be real witches.

'Fancy your chances, then?' Mr Meers watched her, guessing her thoughts. 'Even if you could remember a Spell that long . . . Well, dragons aren't what you'd call friendly. The one in the cave's in the middle of its five-year nap and that makes them really snappy. It might not want to lend you its fire.'

'If I can't say the Spell, I'll never know, will I?' Katy's throat hurt and she looked away. 'I wish I could read like everyone else.'

'I used to think that, myself.' He prodded the sparrow back on to his hat, waiting until it scrambled over the twigs and settled. 'I've never managed to read at all, you know. That's how I lost my Wizard's Licence. I got one Spell too many wrong. Turned the vicar into a schmoo. People didn't like that much.'

'Mr Meers!' Katy gazed at him, horrified. 'You lost a Wizard's licence! I didn't know!'

'Not many people do.'

'But all this . . . You're a magic gardener.' She pointed to the weedless rows of vegetables, the prize-winning fruit. 'You know all the Garden Spells, and some of those are pages long. If you can't read . . .?'

'I remember them.' He winked at his pair of crows and they chuckled back. 'And I'll tell you how, young Katy Wells. I sing 'em.'

'Sing 'em?' Katy stared at him. 'Sing Spells?'

'It's easy, once you're used to it. Just think up a good tune and put the words to it.' Mr Meers scowled at the school roof for a moment. 'You know, it's funny. I can't recite any poetry-thingies but I can remember every song I've ever sung. You sing that Spell, Katy. And we'll see what the dragon says to that.'

Katy sniffed. 'When he hears my voice, he'll probably burn me to a crisp.'

At three o'clock, the girls jiggled into pairs behind Mrs Batsleer's dinosaur, for once too scared to play around or even talk. Fingers crossed, necks hung with as many good-luck charms as they could carry, the girls said goodbye to the other teachers and set off through the town centre, a blue-uniform caterpillar. The people pushed out of their houses to watch or pressed their faces to office windows. No one was sure whether to wave and smile or not, it was so serious. The dragon might decide that they were its supper and not wait to hear the Spell.

Along the canal path, through the thousand-year-old wood where Mrs Batsleer cut mistletoe. Up the hill to the black triangle of the cave mouth. Mrs Batsleer lined the girls up in the order of their last Spelling test. The best first, so that the dragon didn't eat the bad Spellers for nothing. She would have tried herself, but the rules said only a girl between ten and thirteen could charm a dragon.

Mrs Batsleer turned the dinosaur towards the waiting girls and smiled down on them. 'Now, one by one. In you go, Janice.'

Janice Parker cringed. 'Yes, Mrs Batsleer.' She crept into the darkness.

Five minutes later, Janice crept back out, her straw hat swirling in soot flakes, like a halo. 'It didn't work,' she said, and sat on the grass.

'No. Well, if at first you don't succeed . . .' Mrs Batsleer shrugged. 'Next.' Her dinosaur's tail lassoed the girl before she could run away and pulled her back. Mrs Batsleer showed her teeth. 'In you go, Lucy. Try smiling at him.'

Five minutes . . .

'I smiled.' Lucy opened her mouth and bared

19

soot-black gums. 'I don't think he liked it.'

The sounds of a tired dragon losing its temper got louder as each girl crawled through the low crack in the rock. In the end, the girls had to yell the words at the top of their voices and the dragon's snarls made the rocks shudder.

'By the time I get in, it'll be deaf,' Katy moaned. 'I can't even remember the tune, I'm so scared . . .'

'Well.' Mrs Batsleer peered down from her dinosaur. No one else was unsooted except Katy Wells and her mouth twisted with worry. The other girls blinked up at her from the grass like a line of toasted crumpets. Finally, she cleared her throat. 'Well, we didn't do all that well, did we, girls? Katherine, do you still want to try?'

'Yes, Mrs Batsleer.'

'Good girl. Very good girl.' Mrs Batsleer cleared her throat, again. 'In you go, then. And good luck.'

Luck! A fifty-girl sigh, gritty with singed school uniforms, followed Katy into the black tunnel. The low roof meant she had to lie on her stomach and wriggle over the crunch of soot and cinder. Dragon caves ponged. Or maybe cave dragons ponged? Katy slid on a shoe that one of the other girls had left behind, the leather furred with ashes. Then something humphed. At the far end of the dark hole sat a very angry dragon, nostrils snorting sparks, tail twitching against the rock. It was a fine animal, green-scaled with a short beard under its chin and red, burning eyes. Its five-clawed feet glinted pure gold when they crunched the stones. Then the dragon saw her and muttered something unfriendly.

'I'm sorry. But I'm the last one . . .' The dragon blew green fire through its nostrils, stubbornly refusing to listen. 'All right then. Be like that. But I'm still going to try.' Katy closed her eyes and croaked into song.

The words of the Spell echoed around the cave to the tune of 'There's a Worm at the Bottom of my Garden', because it was the only song that fitted. Ten verses, Katy's fingers locked under her chin, eyes aching to open and peek. Every time she breathed in, she tasted soot.

Silence. Katy slowly opened her eyes and squinted into the darkness. The dragon had gone.

'It's not fair . . .' She swallowed and had to cough

and spit soot. 'It isn't. He could have stayed and listened . . .'

'Who told you to sing?' the dragon asked.

'Yiii! Hoo . . .' Katy's voice died.

Nose to nose with her, the dragon gave a smoky humph. Like Mr Meers. 'None of the others did.' It plodded back to its nest of branches and burrowed into them, muttering, 'Like twittering birds. And they all missed the bit about the great cold and the great fire. I like that bit best.'

Katy spluttered. 'Do you?'

The dragon's long mouth curled, nastily. 'Want some fire, then?'

'Please.' Katy tried not to sound desperate, in case it was playing with her. She did not trust that curly mouth. 'It's for the town. To stop their luck running out.'

'Hen piddle.' The dragon snorted a cotton-ball of smoke. 'Superstitious twaddle. Luck from dragon's fire? You might as well get gold from a turnip.'

'But it must be true!' Katy slumped back against the wall. 'The little girl brought the fire . . . And the fire brought the luck . . .'

'Hen piddle.' The dragon made itself comfortable. 'But I suppose that's what people want. Something they can see with their own eyes . . . It's you who has the luck, you know.'

'Me!' Katy goggled. 'Got luck?'

The dragon nodded. 'Like she had, all those years ago. But she was only a skinny little girl, like you. She couldn't even read and no one would have believed her if she'd said she could give them luck. So, she gave them dragon's fire and they believed that. As soon as the fire blew out, they stopped believing.' It scratched behind its left ear with one claw. 'Funny, you both singing the Spell . . .'

Katy smiled, thinking about that little girl, a hundred years ago. A little girl who could not read . . . like Katy, now. 'No it isn't funny. It's because that's how we remembered the words. She was dyslexic, like me. I know she was. Thank you for the fire . . .' She looked at the red eyes. 'If you haven't changed your mind?'

She took her sock off and the dragon humphed.

'Just as long as you don't make a habit of it.' He looked at her, rudely, hot eyes running from her sooty hair to her ash-dusted shoes. 'No, I don't suppose they'll believe you've got luck, either. You're another skinny little girl. But we'll know, won't we?' He breathed a small, green flame into the bottom of the sock, then watched Katy slither away. When she was almost invisible, he sniffed. 'How did that song go . . .?'

Mrs Batsleer's dinosaur plunged, wildly, as a roaring, gargling howl echoed from the cave – like a concrete mixer eating a tree.

'What's that?' She clung to the dinosaur's neck. 'Katy? Did you get the fire? . . . What on earth's that dragon doing in there?'

Katy tied a knot in the top of her sock to stop the fire going out. And grinned. 'He's just singing.' And she started to walk back towards the town, the sock tucked into her skirt pocket, singing,

23

'There's a worm at the bottom of my garden . . .
And his name is Wiggley Wooooo . . .'

She would sing all of her Spells from now on and
be a good witch and give the town all the luck it
needed. And suddenly she knew no one was going
to think she was stupid any more, just because she
couldn't read. From now on, she would tell them.
I'm not stupid! She had brought the dragon's fire
and she had luck inside her and what was inside
her was what counted. Dragons knew that. Only
people could not understand.

The Pigeon

ALISON PRINCE

Outside the minibus windows, trees went past. That meant they were getting near the riding place, Jamie thought, and felt an uneasy shiver run through him at the thought of being lifted on to the pony. It was so high up, and so wobbly.

'Nearly there,' said Mrs Drew in a voice full of promise. Some of the children cheered. The shiver ran through Jamie again, making him want to press his hands together and take a deep breath. But because his hands would never quite do what he told them, they met in an untidy smack, and the breath he took in escaped from him in a meaningless sound he had not meant to utter.

Mrs Drew smiled at him. 'Are you excited, Jamie?' she asked kindly. 'Are you clapping your hands? You like the ponies, don't you?'

No, Jamie wanted to say, he did not like the ponies. Their big, rough strength frightened him and so did the leathery-smelling saddle which creaked under him as the pony moved. It seemed extraordinary to be higher up than the heads of the girls who walked beside him, though he knew it was kind of them to be there, holding a handful of his anorak to make sure he didn't fall off.

Most of the children were clapping excitedly now, as the minibus came to a stop in the stable yard. Some of them were bouncing up and down on the red plastic seats. The rear doors were opened, and smiling girls stood outside. They wore headscarves and practical clothes, and Jamie found them almost as frightening as the ponies. They gave off the same feeling of immense energy, and he knew they were being very good and very patient, giving up a whole morning to Riding For The Disabled. When he had clambered out, with one of the girls holding his arm, he stared down at the grass and wished he was somewhere else.

'Now,' said Mrs Drew, 'we'll have to go in two lots, won't we. Who wants to be first?'

'Me! Me!' Hands shot up. Jamie looked away across the field to where the trees grew. He liked the trees. He liked their quiet rustling, and the way the sky shone between them in little speckles of light, and he liked the spicy smells of long grass and bracken. When they had come last time, in the autumn, Mrs Drew had taken the second group for a walk in the wood to look for brambles while they were waiting for their turn to ride. He hoped she would do it again today.

The first group was hoisted on to the ponies, and the unsteady procession set off slowly across the grass. Mrs Drew went over to the minibus and got out a large red ball. Jamie's heart sank. They were not going to the wood.

'We'll have a game of Rollerball,' Mrs Drew announced. 'Everyone get into a circle. Come along, Mandy. Come along, Jamie.'

Jamie allowed himself to be chivvied gently into

the circle of children. The game was very simple, the object being to keep the ball moving to and fro across the circle by pushing or kicking it. 'Good!' called Mrs Drew. 'Well done, Peter! Lovely!'

The ball came tumbling towards Jamie, bouncing over the tufts of grass. He could imagine himself catching it and rolling it back across the circle while Mrs Drew smiled, but somehow he was looking at the trees again, and the ball had gone past him, and Laura had run to fetch it. Laura was good at running.

Jamie began to feel miserable. He didn't mind about not catching the ball – it seemed odd to him that anyone should bother about whether a ball was caught or not. But standing in a circle was boring, and the grass was muddy, and a cold March wind blew across the field. He heard himself making a disgruntled moaning sound.

Suddenly a commotion broke out on the far side of the circle. Somebody was lying on the grass and Peter was shouting something about Mandy. Mrs Drew was among them quickly, being very calm, bending over Mandy, who was having a fit, Jamie recognised. It happened quite often. He moved off towards the trees. For a little while, nobody would bother about what he was doing.

Staring up through the trees, Jamie thought the whole sky seemed to be hurrying sideways. White clouds rushed across its blueness, and the thin branches seemed to be caught up with the clouds, dragged by the wind until they whipped back, only to be caught and dragged again. It was all very exciting. In the school, when you looked up, there were only ceilings. Jamie felt a wild impulse to dance, and his arms reached out and waved about like the tree branches, but then he lost his balance and was suddenly sprawled on the damp ground, among the brown leaves and the long, soft grass.

With some difficulty, Jamie managed to get to his feet. He stood there, lurching and breathless after his fall. Quite suddenly, he felt furiously angry with his scarecrow body which would not move in the smooth, well-ordered way which other people took for granted. He thought of the ordeal of the pony ride which lay ahead, and of the days beyond that, filled with boredom because he could never tell anyone what his thoughts were, and so they treated him as if he was stupid. His shoulders twisted themselves with the irritation he felt, and his arms flailed about so that he almost fell down again.

You great twit, Jamie said to himself in careful, scornful words. There's no point in standing here, carrying on like a clown, wasting time. They'll be looking for you, once Mandy comes round from her fit. Once they start the game again.

He took a few more steps into the wood. Then he heard a strange sound – a brief fluttering of wings which stopped again almost at once. It was like the starlings which flew up from the lawn outside the school when Mrs Drew opened the front door, only much closer. The sound came again, and this time Jamie saw what it was. In the criss-crossing twigs of a hazel tree, a bird was dangling untidily by one

foot which was trapped in the overlap of two branches. Once again, the wings flapped convulsively then stopped, hanging down as if the bird was too exhausted to fold them.

Jamie stared, fascinated and dismayed. The bird was a pigeon of some kind, pearly grey in colour, with a dark band round the base of its neck. He could see how the crossing of the branches held the pink leg imprisoned. If someone could pull the nearer branch away from the other one, the gap would open and the bird would be free. From habit, Jamie glanced round for help. From between the trees, he could see the group of children clustered round Mrs Drew, who was still crouching beside Mandy. He looked back at the bird, and felt hot all over as he realised that this was something he would have to do himself.

It was terribly hard to persuade his hands to come together round the thin branch of the tree. When he got one of them, it would jerk away again before he could get the other one organised and his wayward legs were no help, shifting erratically at just the wrong time. Tears of frustration sprang to Jamie's eyes and he snarled furiously at himself, his face contorted with effort. He had never worked so hard.

Suddenly, it all came together. Both hands were on the branch at the same moment, and a lucky sagging of the knees threw his whole weight on the branch. It gave way at once, bending easily towards him, and Jamie fell backwards, collapsing again on to the ground.

He lay there, panting. Above him, the trees swung to and fro across the sky as his head turned from side to side. He could not see the pigeon. Laboriously, he managed to roll on his side – and found the bird lying on the leaves, quite close to him. Its beak was slightly open, and the feathers on its chest puffed quickly up and down with its breathing. The leg which had been trapped stuck out awkwardly behind it, but as Jamie watched, it drew the foot up to its body and clenched the pink claws into a little fist, then spread them again. He had never seen a bird at such close quarters before. He gazed at the yellow-ringed, wide-open eye and the neat head, the grey plumage and the long, sweeping feathers of the wing, and longed to touch it.

The bird did not move as Jamie, with a tremendous effort of will, managed to bring his hand across to it. He gave its feathers a single trembling stroke before his wayward arm jerked away again. The other one was pinned below him as he lay uncomfortably on the ground.

'Jamie! Where are you?' Mrs Drew's distant voice sounded anxious. 'Jamie?'

Jamie did not want her to be worried. He tried to shout, 'I'm over here!' but it came out as an inarticulate yell, as usual. That was the worst of it, he thought, the stupid noises he made. You couldn't blame people for thinking he was an idiot. He set about the business of getting up.

By the time Mrs Drew reached him, he was on his feet and making his way out of the wood. He had not dared to try and pick the pigeon up in case he accidentally hurt it, so he had left it crouched among the brown leaves. He could still feel the touch of its feathers on his fingers, a tingle which went on being exciting. He would think about that in bed tonight, he promised himself, that lovely moment of stroking the pigeon. It was something to look forward to. But now, there was Mrs Drew.

'Jamie, what *have* you been doing? Just look at your trousers! Earth all over you!' She picked a dead leaf from his hair, and brushed at him with her hand. 'Come along. Your pony's waiting for you.'

As they hoisted him into the saddle and

arranged his feet in the stirrups, Jamie thought of the pigeon, hanging helplessly upside-down with its wings beating at the air. Wobbling about on a pony was not as bad as that, he told himself. For the first time, he felt quite lucky.

'Grab a handful of his mane,' one of the girls walking beside him urged. 'Like this, look. You won't hurt him, it's all right.' She captured Jamie's wandering right hand and pushed it down to the pony's neck, and he felt his fingers entangle with the coarse, dark hair. Unexpectedly, he found himself liking the sensation. It was almost as nice as the touch of the pigeon's feathers. He remembered how he had made his hands come together round the tree branch, and laughed with triumph. He had done it. He had released the bird.

With the thought of release, his hand let go of the pony's mane. Jamie struggled to bring it back again. First one hand, then the other. They did not stay all the time, but they kept coming back to enjoy the feeling of the thick strands of hair. And the pony was walking forward. Jamie laughed again. It was all right. He was not going to fall off. He was riding the pony and the clouds were blowing merrily across the blue sky. If I had been born a pigeon, he thought, I would know how to fly. It's just luck, the way things are.

Back in the stable yard, the girls lifted him down, and Jamie immediately set off across the grass towards the trees.

'Jamie, where are you going?' called Mrs Drew from the minibus, where she sat beside Mandy.

Jamie turned awkwardly and explained that he wouldn't be long, but with no real hope that she would understand him.

'Sylvia, go with him, dear, could you?' said Mrs Drew. 'He seems to be very fascinated with the trees, I don't know why. Just take him for a little walk over there and bring him straight back.'

'Okay,' said the girl obligingly. 'Come on, sunshine.' She took Jamie's hand and led him across the grass. It would have been nicer to go on his own, Jamie thought, but he was used to having people with him all the time, and didn't mind much.

'Here we are,' said the girl as they reached the wood. 'They're nice trees, aren't they? Do you like trees?'

Jamie tried to nod and say 'Yes,' but it came out as 'Ah.'

The girl smiled at him, still holding his hand. 'I like trees too,' she said. 'Specially the ones that have pink flowers on them in the spring. Japanese cherries, they're called. We've got one in our garden.'

Jamie was not listening. He saw the hazel tree, with the branch he had pulled down still leaning towards him. He twisted his hand away from Sylvia's grip and lurched a couple of paces forward to where he had left the bird crouching in the leaves. There was no sign of it.

In a way, Jamie was disappointed. He had wanted to see it again, to assure himself that it was real, for now it was beginning to seem like

33

some wild kind of dream that he had managed to give the pigeon its freedom, and that he had stroked its grey feathers. And yet, he told himself, it had gone because it felt strong enough to fly away. It was a proper bird again, living in the trees and the sky.

'What are you looking for?' asked Sylvia. 'There's no brambles, not in March.' She reached up to the hazel tree and picked off a small grey feather which clung to the bark. 'Have this instead,' she offered, catching his hand and putting the feather between fingers and thumb. 'Okay?'

Jamie was filled with delight. It was like a little

present from the pigeon, to say thank you. The girl
led him back across the field. Then the feather
slipped from Jamie's grasp and he uttered a
scream of dismay as the wind caught it and
whirled it away.

'I'll get it!' said Sylvia, and rushed after it. Jamie
waited, shaking with anxiety, until she recaptured
the feather and brought it back to him. This time,
she tucked it into his anorak pocket. 'There!' she
said. 'Okay?'

Jamie smiled. It was very okay. He thought
about the word. 'Kay,' he said, and laughed with
surprise because it sounded so like what the girl
had said.

'Okay,' agreed Sylvia, not knowing it was the
first intelligible word he had spoken. 'Okay, okay.'

Mrs Drew smiled at Jamie as she helped him
into the bus. 'Was it nice in the wood?' she asked.

Jamie's smile faded for a moment. He wished he
could explain about finding the pigeon, and about
the triumph of managing to set it free, and how
the pony ride had been all right, and how the
feather, a tiny part of the bird itself, was safe in his
anorak pocket. But it didn't really matter. All
these lovely things had happened, and that was
enough. He smiled again. *'Kay,'* he said.

Beggar Your Neighbour

CAREY BLYTON

When Sulochana Gunetillaka had polio it seemed that all his hopes were dashed. He was off school for a year, learning to walk again and coming to terms with his handicap – a withered leg which he could walk on but which he dragged behind him slowly and laboriously.

Once he was back with his family, there was no question of his continuing his schooling. The school was in another district of Colombo, and it was too far away to walk to it or even take the bus. He would not have been able to fight his way, twice a day, on to the always over-crowded buses that tore along Galle Road, jam-packed with people and with late-comers hanging on to the bus doors for dear life. He tried it just once and was thrown to the ground and left bruised and bleeding in the gutter while the bus rushed off leaving him behind.

What was even worse, the job at a coconut plantation a few miles north of Colombo, which his father had arranged for him to go to when he left school, was also out of the question. Even if he could have got to the plantation, there was no way that he could join the other boys and young men who harvested the coconuts, climbing up the slim, smooth trunks to a height of twenty, thirty or more feet to chop the ripe fruit off the crowns of the trees with a machete.

His family was poor. His father had a job as a gardener in a rich part of Colombo, but it paid little. His mother did laundry for a nearby hotel, a job with long, hard hours for very little money. His brothers and sisters had all left home, either because they had married or had jobs which took them to other parts of the Island to live and work. He had been a late arrival; he was just fourteen years old, and the next above him was his sister, Delani, who was twenty-six. Sulochana knew that his mother and father had looked forward to the time when he would start to earn money, so that all their lives would become easier. Now it looked instead as though he would be a burden to them.

One day, a day he would always remember, his father spoke to him after their evening meal. He was clearly unhappy and embarrassed.

'Sulochana, you know that your mother and I were looking forward to the time you would start earning money. We are neither of us getting any younger, and some extra money every week would be such a help to us.'

His father looked at him to see if he had anything to say, but Sulochana could think of nothing, so he remained silent. His father continued.

'We have discussed things a great deal, and we think there is nothing left now but for you to beg for money, as you cannot work at a proper job. We are sorry, really we are. But you could go each day to the market or sit outside a big bank or a big hotel. That way, you could get a little money.'

Sulochana still said nothing, but his thoughts were racing. A beggar? He could hardly bear to think of it. To join the lepers without noses, or fingers, the blind people, and those without arms and legs who begged outside the banks and hotels. It was too horrible to think about, and Sulochana felt his eyes filling with tears. His father noticed and looked away.

'I know it's a terrible thing. And I wouldn't ask this of you except that I worry about Mother. I would so like to see her give up her work at the hotel laundry or, at any rate, spend less time there. If you could bring back a little money each day, this would be possible.'

Sulochana said nothing. His father rose and, as he left the tiny room that served as both living-room and bedroom, he squeezed Sulochana's shoulder in passing. Sulochana sat for a long time thinking about what might have been, about going to the end of his schooling, about the coconut plantation and about how unfair life was. Now that his father had gone he let the tears trickle slowly down his face and drop on to the old worn rush-matting of the room. He felt quite numb and unable to move.

It was several days before Sulochana could bring himself to 'go to work'. Then, one hot, bright morning, he dragged himself out of the house, down the lane to the main road to join the beggars outside the bank, each hoping to get a few coins from the people going in and out.

He found a space near the steps and looked around at his new neighbours. There was an old man with only one eye, the other eye's socket covered with a piece of cloth that flapped in the breeze. There was a blind boy, with a white stick and a placard round his neck which said: 'Blind from Birth' in English, Sinhala and Tamil. And there was also a strange man Sulochana had seen many times before who had no legs, and who sat in a sort of wooden box on little wheels. He propelled himself about in this curious conveyance using his hands on the ground, the knuckles of each hand wrapped in cloth to protect them from the rough pavements. There was also a woman with a crutch who had one foot missing.

In a curious way Sulochana felt a little encouraged, since his own handicap seemed to be much less severe than the others'. But he soon found that this worked to his disadvantage, since those people who put coins into the beggars' bowls tended to put them in the bowls of the most seriously handicapped, and not very often into his.

He found it a long, hot day, and very tiring. Around midday he ate the small handful of rice and the mango his mother had given him before she left for work. Several of the other beggars asked him to share his food with them, and he shared round the little he had. The man in the box thanked him very gravely but silently with a salaam, the palms of his hands together and the hands brought up to touch his chest. At three

o'clock the bank shut and the other beggars moved
off. Sulochana guessed they were going to beg
outside one of the big hotels where the tourists
stayed or at the nearby market. But he was so
tired and hungry that all he could do was to limp
slowly back home, dragging his leg wearily behind
him. There, although he was hungry, he just fell
into a deep sleep, exhausted both mentally and
physically from his first day's work.

When his father came home from work,
Sulochana woke up and gave him the money he
had begged: three rupees and seventy-five cents.
Hardly a fortune, but enough to pay for a meal.
His father took the money without saying
anything.

As the days passed, Sulochana became used to
the routine, and after a few weeks he knew who
were the bank's regular customers – shopkeepers,
local businessmen, hotel staff and the tourist office
people, who came with Westerners to help them
change their money and travellers' cheques. He
could recognise one or two of the policemen who
stood on duty at the entrance to the bank. And he
also got to know Mr Carrim.

Mr Carrim was a Sri Lankan of Malayan des-
cent, a tall, handsome man of about fifty, with an
upright, military bearing, who was employed by
the bank to act as a kind of public relations man.
One of the other beggars told Sulochana that Mr
Carrim had been in the army in his youth, at the
time of the British Raj. When a prospective cus-
tomer – or, more usually, a Westerner – entered

the bank and looked around helplessly, wondering which counter to go to, Mr Carrim came forward briskly and efficiently and helped them. He spoke excellent English and soon sorted out any problems. Although he never gave money to any of the beggars, he was quite friendly towards them, only becoming rather fierce and angry if any beggar dared to sit on the steps or tried to enter the bank itself. And he always had a smile for Sulochana who, although he felt drawn to Mr Carrim, was a little overawed by him.

For Sulochana, the best day of the week was Thursday, when money was delivered to the bank. A Securi-Co van would draw up outside the bank at 9.45 am precisely and the policeman on duty would stand with his rifle at the ready, just to one side of the main entrance. Two men got out of the van with the money, well protected with crash-helmets and with the money in attaché cases manacled to their wrists by means of chains. The driver of the van stood by the van, holding a shotgun. He, too, wore a crash-helmet. It was all very exciting and Sulochana was always sorry that each Thursday, just before the van arrived, the policeman and Mr Carrim would make him and the other beggars move off, away from the bank entrance.

The bank was situated at a cross-roads and at one side was a narrow side-street. The side-street was always a mess, with lots of old boxes and crates piled up in the hope – not often realized – that the dustmen would take them away. Outside

one shop, 'Mallika Batik', there were always huge piles of large cardboard boxes, in a great jumble. Sulochana would usually go there in the heat of the day to find some shade, or when the Securi-Co van called at the bank and there were no customers going in and out because of the money delivery.

One day, sheltering from the midday sun behind the pile of boxes, Sulochana heard a very strange conversation coming from an open window just above him. A man was speaking:

'. . . no problem. They never worry about the side-entrance. It'll be easy to enter the bank at ten, when they open, lure the policeman into the bank and silence him, and then shut and lock the main doors. We can put up a notice – BANK OPENING AT ELEVEN or something – to keep people away. Sunil can have the get-away car at the side-entrance. I tell you, I've been over this a dozen times. It's foolproof.'

Another voice answered, but it was too far away for Sulochana to hear very clearly what it said.

Sulochana held his breath, straining with all his might to hear. Then the first voice said very clearly: 'Okay. Then we do it next Thursday – and don't forget the guns. Get a twelve-bore shot-gun if you can – sawn-off if possible . . .'

The other man grunted and then, without warning, the door of 'Mallika Batik' suddenly opened. Sulochana pressed himself back against the wall, hiding behind the pile of boxes. Through a chink in them he saw the two men leave the shop. One he did not know, but the other man he recognised immediately. He had seen him going in and out of the bank many times over the past weeks. He was about thirty and well-dressed in Western clothes. The other man wore a sarong.

They disappeared from view, going down the side-street towards the sea. Sulochana sat there with his heart pounding. He did not know what to do. His first thought was to get into the bank somehow and warn them. But then he realized it would be difficult to get in without Mr Carrim stopping him. Mr Carrim . . . Suddenly he had an idea.

He made his way back to the bank entrance.

Most of the usual beggars were there and he joined them. The morning seemed to pass very slowly and he kept looking into the bank to make sure Mr Carrim was there. He was. Then, at midday, his usual time, Mr Carrim came out of the bank to go for his lunch. Sulochana spoke to him.

'Mr Carrim?'

Mr Carrim stopped and looked at him in surprise.

'Mr Carrim. Please may I speak to you for a moment?'

The tall Malay eyed Sulochana for a moment. There was something in Sulochana's face and voice that told him it was important.

'Okay. But not here. Can you get to the "Maliban Kreme House"? That's where I have my lunch. You can talk to me while I eat.'

Sulochana lurched after Mr Carrim, picking his way carefully over Galle Road's broken paving-stones. When they came to the restaurant, a waiter tried to stop Sulochana from entering. Mr Carrim waved him aside.

'It's okay. He's with me. I will vouch for him.'

The waiter stood aside reluctantly and they made their way to a table near the window. Mr Carrim sat down and, realising that Sulochana was still standing awkwardly by the chair opposite him, motioned to him to sit down. Sulochana sat down, perching on the very edge of the seat. Mr Carrim looked at the menu.

When the waiter came he ordered two chicken *lamprais*. Sulochana was embarrassed.

'Please, Mr Carrim, I wanted to speak to you, not beg a meal from you.'

Mr Carrim smiled.

'Well, I can hardly eat alone in front of you. And I expect you could eat something now – I don't suppose you had much for breakfast.'

Sulochana nodded but said nothing. When the food came, Mr Carrim began eating. Sulochana was too excited to eat straight away and started to tell him what he had overheard. Mr Carrim did not interrupt him once but listened thoughtfully. When Sulochana had finished, Mr Carrim said:

'You say you recognised the younger man, the one in Western clothes?'

'Yes.'

'Describe him to me again.'

Sulochana did so, adding, this time, that the man wore a tie, a rather bright and gaudy tie which looked American.

'Ah, yes,' said Mr Carrim, 'I know the man now. He's been in many times recently.'

He called the waiter over and took the bill from its little saucer. He turned to Sulochana and said very quietly:

"Now. You are to say nothing to anyone. Do you understand? No one. Not even your mother and father or to any of your family. Just leave everything to me. Okay?"

Sulochana nodded his head vigorously but said nothing. Mr Carrim got up and went over to the cashier and paid the bill. He came back to Sulochana, who was still sitting at the table.

'It's best we leave separately. I'll go first and then you leave after about five minutes. Okay?'

Sulochana nodded again and just sat there, watching Mr Carrim leave, his upright bearing making him look very much like a soldier on the parade-ground. Mr Carrim disappeared from view and Sulochana sat for a few minutes, lost in thought. He suddenly realised that he hadn't even thanked Mr Carrim for the food.

After a little while he left the restaurant and made his way back, slowly and carefully, to the bank steps and sat down with the other beggars. His mind was racing. He wanted to tell his neighbours all about the planned robbery but knew he must say nothing to anyone. He felt as though he would burst with excitement.

He went home as soon as the bank shut and sat in the little front room in a daze. When his father came home from work Sulochana didn't even answer him when he said: 'Hello! Did you have an interesting day, Sulochana?'

The next days passed very slowly and Sulochana felt himself wishing the time away to the coming Thursday, when the robbery was planned to take place. When the day finally came, he left home very early in the morning and was the first beggar to be outside the bank. It was a little before nine o'clock – about three-quarters of an hour before the Securi-Co van would come with the money.

The other beggars arrived, one by one, and took up their places near the steps. At half-past nine the policeman arrived and took up his position just outside the bank doors, which were still locked. Sulochana tried hard not to stare at him. Surely it was one of the men he had seen leaving 'Mallika Batik'. What did it mean? Where was the real policeman? Sulochana's heart was pounding. He wondered if he ought to warn Mr Carrim, who he could see moving about inside the bank through the glass doors.

At 9.45 precisely, the Securi-Co van arrived. The policeman sprang to attention with his rifle ready. Mr Carrim unlocked the bank doors and opened them and the two Securi-Co men, with attaché cases manacled to their wrists, entered the bank. They came out after about five minutes, entered the van and drove off. Sulochana's mouth was quite dry. Then the policeman entered the bank and the doors were locked again. Already, a number of prospective customers were gathering, waiting for the bank to open at ten o'clock.

Suddenly, Sulochana noticed that the other of the two men he had seen leaving 'Mallika Batik' was in the little queue, waiting for the bank to open. He had a briefcase with him which seemed to be very full. Mr Carrim appeared behind the glass doors of the bank and opened them. The waiting customers entered the bank – perhaps six or seven people all told. After a minute or so the man with the briefcase appeared at the bank entrance and shut and locked the doors.

He placed a large sign on the inside of one of the doors so that it could be read easily from the street. It said:

BANK WILL OPEN AT ELEVEN TODAY.

Then, without warning, two cars hurtled up the road. One turned into the side-street and the other screeched to a half in front of the bank. Three uniformed policemen leapt out and suddenly Mr Carrim appeared behind the bank doors and unlocked them. The three policemen pushed through the doors. Minutes later the robbers were being bundled into the police car and it was all over.

Mr Carrim appeared at the top of the steps and beckoned Sulochana to come up and enter the bank. He did so, very slowly and carefully. Inside the bank felt deliciously cool after the heat outside. Mr Carrim motioned for Sulochana to follow him and led the way to a door marked: REGINALD DE SILVA, Manager. He followed Mr Carrim into the office where the manager was sitting at the desk. Mr Carrim indicated to Sulochana that he should sit down.

'I expect you are wondering what happened in here this morning, yes?'

Sulochana nodded.

'I'll leave Mr Carrim to tell it. It's really his story.'

'Well, there's not a lot to tell,' said Mr Carrim. 'Thanks to you, we knew who to expect. As soon as I saw the 'policeman' I knew we had to deal with three men at least: the young man with the gaudy tie, the man in the get-away car and the 'policeman'. Once the Securi-Co men had gone, our little gang started work! Mr Gaudy Tie produced a sawn-off shot-gun from his briefcase and tried to hold us up. But he hadn't reckoned with all the police in the bank! Six of the 'customers' were armed plainclothes-men, to say nothing of the dozen armed, uniformed men who were in hiding, below the level of the counters. You would've liked to see the expression on Mr Gaudy Tie's face, once he realised they were outnumbered by about ten to one! And when his get-away driver appeared from the back of the bank, already arrested and handcuffed to a policeman, he knew that the game was up. The battle was lost without a single shot being fired . . . thank goodness. That's about all there was to it, really.'

Sulochana wished so much that he could have seen it all. But it was still very exciting. He could hardly wait to get home and tell his mother and father all about it.

'It was the bank's intention to give you a reward for your help,' said the manager, 'but Mr Carrim has had another idea. I would like to come and see your parents this evening, if that is possible, to talk to them about it.'

Sulochana was lost for words for a moment. Then he mumbled confusedly: 'Yes, sir. Of course, sir.'

'I expect Mr de Silva has a lot to do now,' said Mr Carrim, 'so we will go for lunch – and you can give me your address.'

It seemed an age before his mother returned from her work at the hotel and a little later, his father

came in. Sulochana poured out the whole story to his amazed parents, who just sat and stared at him without speaking. Promptly at six o'clock, Mr Carrim and Mr de Silva arrived by car. After introductions were made, Mr de Silva came straight to the point.

'As a token of our appreciation for what Sulochana has done, Mr Carrim has suggested – and the bank has agreed – that, if he so wishes, he can come to work at the bank. Mr Carrim says he will take him under his wing, and help him all he can. We have in mind a desk job, of course, nothing that would involve any walking about. If you agree, Sulochana could start next Monday. The salary would be two hundred rupees a month and, of course, he would get all the normal benefits that the other bank employees get – luncheon vouchers, paid holidays and so on.'

Sulochana and his parents sat quite stunned. Two hundred rupees a month! It would make all the difference in the world to their lives. Sulochana's father spoke:

'I don't know what to say. I mean . . . it's such a surprise . . . a shock.'

Sulochana's mother broke in practically:

'Thank you, Mr de Silva. I'm sure Sulochana would be very happy to work for you. Isn't that right, Sulochana?'

Sulochana nodded, still unable to say a word. Mr de Silva stood up.

'Right. I'll see you then, Sulochana, on Monday morning at nine o'clock sharp – I'm afraid we start work a bit before the bank opens at ten!' He smiled.

Sulochana's parents saw Mr de Silva to the car and, as Sulochana walked towards it with Mr Carrim, he said to him:

'I don't know how to thank you, Mr Carrim. I never expected—'

Mr Carrim interrupted him, looking at him quizzically with his head on one side:

'One good turn deserves another,' he said. Sulochana looked at him inquiringly.

'You probably didn't see, but I saw you – the first day you appeared outside the bank. I saw you share your food with the other beggars – even

though you had so little. I decided then and there
that I'd help you if I could – and your own honesty
and concern for the bank made it possible. That's
all there is to it.'

He looked away uncomfortably for a moment,
and then added:

'Don't let me down now. Be at the bank on
Monday in good time . . . or else!'

As he drove off he turned and waved. Sulochana
and his parents returned to the little front room
and, his heart so filled with joy, Sulochana
grabbed his mother's wrists and whirled her round
and round, hopping on his good leg. Without
warning he caught his foot on the mat and fell, his
mother sprawled on top of him. He just laughed
and shouted: 'I've got a job! I've got a job!' And he
scooped the old rush mat up into his arms and
threw it high into the air, still laughing. Suddenly
he stopped laughing and said very quietly and
seriously to his parents:

'But the beggars will still be my neighbours.
Maybe I can do more now to help them?'

The Crossing

VIVIEN ALCOCK

The playground was in Highgate Woods, on the other side of the Archway Road. Go out of the garden gate, face left, walk nineteen steps forward and you'd reach the post of the controlled crossing. Press the button and wait. Soon the big trucks, down from the North and up from the docks, would shudder and squeal to a stop. You'd smell dust and diesel, hear them panting and feel the heat on your cheeks. You'd hear the urgent beep-beep-beep, like a frantic blackbird, and you'd know it was safe to cross. Easy.

'You don't have to come with me,' Jake told his sister, trying not to sound irritable, for it was her birthday and he had promised Dad he would be nice to her all day. 'I can go by myself. I asked Dad. He said yes.'

'Did you ask Mum?' Susan demanded. 'I bet you didn't. She'd have said no. She worries about you. Like I do. I don't mind taking you.'

'I thought you wanted to go to Oxford Street, to buy that new dress for your party tonight,' he said, but it was no good.

'I'll take you there on my way and one of your friends can bring you back,' she said.

'Don't ask them,' he begged. 'I'm not a baby. I'm supposed to do things for myself.'

'Not today. Not for the first time on my birthday. I wouldn't have an easy moment. It would spoil my afternoon. Please, Jake—'

Please be a baby. Please let us wrap you up in cotton wool until we have time to attend to you, he thought bitterly. Why won't they listen to the teachers at my school? Dad does. Dad knows I've got to learn to be independent. I'm not stupid. I wouldn't do anything rash. I'm eleven years old and I'm sick of being fussed over. I wish the holidays were over. I wish I were back at school.

He didn't say any of this aloud, but picked up his stick, Tapitty, in silence and went with her into the summer sunlight. Out of the garden gate, face left, walk nineteen steps forward . . . He could do it in his sleep.

Fuss, fuss, fuss! he thought angrily, swishing Tapitty through the air as if he was cutting off heads – his bossy older sister's head, for a start.

'Careful, Jake,' she said. 'You might hit someone, doing that.'

'I don't see how when there's nobody there,' he said scornfully. 'I'd hear them. I've still got ears, haven't I? Sharper ones than yours. Besides, I'm not quite blind, you know.'

Not quite. He could see, dimly, light and dark, and even colour if it was bright enough. His sister's red dress, beside him, was a faint warm smudge in his shadow world.

'Everyone must be still having lunch,' Susan said when they reached the playground. 'There's hardly anyone here. Dolly Benton and her kid

54

brothers in the sandpit. Ugh! They never wash their feet. I don't think the youngest boy's dry yet either. It's disgusting. He must be nearly five.'

Jake didn't say anything. Susan didn't want him to be friends with Dolly because she said she was rough and used bad words, but Jake liked her. He'd never seen Dolly, for she'd only come to the playground recently, long after his eyes had gone wrong, but he was sure she was pretty. She had a beautiful voice, soft and sweet and a little husky. Sometimes she'd sit on the edge of the sandpit and read to her small brothers, tales of princes and goose-girls and faraway places.

'You like stories?' she asked, the first time she'd noticed he was listening.

'Yes,' he said, 'I've grown out of fairy stories, of course, but I like reading.'

'They teach you that Braille stuff at your school?'

'Yes.'

'Is it difficult?'

'Not really,' he told her. 'It helps if you've got sensitive fingers.' He turned his hands over, palms upwards.

'Gawd, ain't they clean!' she'd cried admiringly, and they both laughed.

'What colour's your hair?' he'd asked her.

'Black. And my eyes are blue. And though I say it meself, I don't look so bad on a Saturday night.'

'Only on Saturday?' he'd asked.

'That's when I have me bath,' she said, and they were still laughing when Susan had come up and

55

taken him away.

'Don't play with her,' Susan had told him. 'I bet she's got nits in her hair. Mum will scalp you if you catch them.'

'I'll be friends with whom I like!' he'd said angrily and they'd had a row about it. But he mustn't quarrel with her today. It was her birthday. He sighed.

I'll go over to Dolly when Susan's gone, he thought.

He turned his head, getting his bearings. He knew this small playground by heart. He had come here with Susan since they were small. It was their playground, almost opposite the house in which they lived. He knew where everything was; the slides, the seesaw, the swings . . .

The big swings were in use, all three of them. He could hear the squeal of their chains on the metal bar, backwards and forwards, going high, higher . . .

'You'll have to wait for the swings,' his sister said. 'There're some people on them. I wonder who they are.'

'Don't know.'

'They're mad. What are they dressed up like that for?'

'Like what?'

'In crash helmets and leather jackets. They must be roasting! Why don't they take them off?'

Jake shrugged.

'I don't like the look of them,' his sister said. 'They're sort of sinister. What are they doing in the playground? They're far too old. Must be seventeen or eighteen, at least. They're much too heavy for those swings. Someone ought to tell them.' She looked round but there were no grown-ups in sight, only Dolly Benton and her small brothers in the sandpit. 'I've a good mind to tell them myself.'

'No, don't, Sue!' Jake pleaded. 'Leave them alone. Anyway, they're stopping now.'

He could hear the swings slowing down, the dragging of feet on the ground acting as brakes. 'You'll wear your shoes out' Susan had always told him when he'd done that.

There was a rattle of chains as the youths got off the swings. Jake heard them whispering together. Two of them wanted to go back to the pub for a bite to eat. 'There's no pickings here,' they said.

'I dunno,' the third one muttered. 'That bird's got a fat-looking bag.'

Who does he mean? Jake wondered. Dolly? Sue? Sue and her birthday money! He heard heavy footsteps coming close. Saw a dark shadow—

'Who d'you think you're staring at?' a loud voice said, hoarse as a crow's.

'Don't answer,' Susan whispered.

'I was talking to you, chick, you in the pillarbox dress,' the hoarse voice cried. 'Ain't your ma told you it's rude to turn your back on people?'

'Don't take any notice,' Susan whispered, but her hand trembled on Jake's arm. A figure brushed roughly between them, smelling of warm leather and sweat and stale tobacco – and

something else, something familiar—'Carry your bag, miss?'

'No,' Susan said. 'Leave it alone!' Her voice rose to a shriek. 'Don't! Don't!'

Jake launched himself at a whirling shadow. His fingers scrabbled on a leather sleeve, clung to a wrist. 'Run, Sue!' he shouted. An arm hit him so violently that he went flying, landing with a jolt that seemed to loosen his brain.

For a moment he didn't know which way up the world was, or even if it was still there. Then he heard Dolly's voice, no longer soft but shrill with anger, shouting,

'You knocked him down! He's blind and you hit

him! I hope God strikes you dead!'

Jake got to his feet, flushing hotly. 'I can look after myself,' he muttered, jerking his arm from her supporting hand, but then had to ask, 'Where's Tappity? Where's my stick?'

She gave it to him, and he stood looking round with his smoky eyes, holding the stick in his hand like a sword, a blind young warrior searching for enemies to fight.

But they had gone, leaping over the low fence round the play ground, running off through the woods and out of sight. There was only Dolly and her kid brothers, and Susan, sitting on a bench and weeping for her lost bag.

'All my money. All gone. Every penny. All my birthday money.'

The others tried to comfort her. 'I got 50p. You can have that,' Dolly told her, and her two little brothers searched their pockets and came up with a squashed toffee which they offered to her and she refused.

'They were going back to a pub. I heard them say so,' Jake said. 'I bet it was the Woodman. I expect they left their bikes in the car-park. Let's go after them.'

'They won't hang about. They'll be gone before we get there.'

'They might not. They were going to eat there. It's worth a try.'

'Even if they were still there, what could we do?'

'I know the landlord there,' Dolly said. 'Mr Wells. He's a friend of me mum's. He'd help us.

And you could phone the police from there.'

The landlord of the Woodman pub stood in the doorway and looked out over the crowded garden. He looked at the young men sitting at the tables. He looked at the crash helmets and leather jackets piled on the end of benches or lying on the ground by their feet.

'There must be a rally somewhere,' he said. 'The place is crawling with them. Same inside. Never seen so many crash helmets before. Leather jackets by the hundred. Take your pick.'

'Them over there,' Dolly said, nodding towards three youths sitting at a table near the lattice fence. 'So Jake says.'

'That's the blind boy?'

'Yes. But he's clever.'

'What does his sister say?'

'Same as me. She dunno. Not to swear to. They were wearing all their gear then, you see. We never saw their faces properly. It could be them. Jake swears to it.'

'I'd better see him then.'

The children were standing on the pavement on the other side of the lattice fence; a girl in a bright red dress, holding Dolly's small brothers by the hands, and a boy of about eleven or twelve, who turned his head as they came up. His eyes were dark and soft. The landlord was a big man and his dog was big, too. Jake held his hand out fearlessly to the Doberman who sniffed his fingers and licked them. Mr Wells would not have known he was blind, except for the stick he carried.

The landlord turned back to the girl. 'I hear you've had your bag stolen?'

'Yes. In the woods. But I don't know—'

'I do,' the boy said firmly, interrupting her. 'It was him. Look through here. You can just see him through the leaves.'

Mr Wells bent down and looked. He could see the table Dolly had pointed out and the three youths sitting in the sun.

'How can you tell?' he asked.

'By his voice. I'd know him anywhere. He sounds hoarse and every now and then, there's a sort of click at the back of his throat. Listen! He's talking now.'

They were silent for a moment.

'I can't hear it,' the landlord said at last. 'But I expect your ears are better than mine.'

'He's got ears like a fox,' Susan said. 'Jake can hear a pin drop in a thunderstorm.'

'Mmm. All right. But I can't afford to make a mistake. Have you anything else to go by?'

'He smelled funny. Like – a sort of hospital smell. Ointment or something . . . And his wrist felt . . . Has he got a bandage on his wrist?'

They all stared through the lattice fence and the thin screen of leaves, stared at the bulky youth, with his thick red arms, now bare, and the grubby white bandage on his left wrist.

'That's good enough for me,' Mr Wells said. 'Jake and – Susan, is it? You come with me. Dolly, stay and look after your brothers.'

'We're all coming,' Dolly said fiercely.

'Keep in the background then, all of you. I don't want anyone getting hurt.'

They went into the pub garden, the landlord and his dog leading the way. The children stopped when they were told and watched Mr Wells and Jasper go up to the table with the three youths. They heard him say politely,

'Good afternoon, gentlemen. I hear you found a girl's bag in the woods. I expect you've been looking for the owner, and I'm glad to tell you she's here. So if you'd like to hand it over, it'll be a happy ending for all concerned, won't it?'

The three youths stared at him silently. Then the bulky one said hoarsely, 'Dunno what you're talking about. We never found nothing, did we?'

His companions shook their heads but glanced uneasily at the children.

'We could, of course,' the landlord said, 'discuss it with the police, if you'd prefer that.'

The bulky youth stared at him, stared past him at the children and past them to the opening beyond. One of his companions muttered something and they looked at the dog. The dog yawned, showing sharp white teeth.

'Who says we found it?' the bulky youth asked.

'You were seen.'

'They couldn't have seen our faces. We was wearing—' the bulky youth broke off and his face crimsoned. He made a sudden movement as if to get to his feet and the dog growled.

'Keep him off! You didn't ought to have a

62

dangerous animal like that loose. It's against the law!'

'Stealing's against the law, too,' Mr Wells said. 'Come on, lad. It's hand it over to me or the police. I don't mind which.'

And that was the end of it. The youths threw the purse on the table, muttering something about the bag being in the litter bin in the car-park, and the landlord, after checking with Susan that all the money was intact, let them go with a warning.

'I don't want to see you around again. Neither in the pub nor in the woods where I walk my dog. I don't think he's taken to you. I don't think he likes you one little bit.'

The youths went off in a hurry, carrying their belongings in their arms, not looking at the children, not looking at anyone. One of them blundered into the table, as if he hadn't seen it, and scattered the uneaten sandwiches all over the grass.

The landlord watched them out of sight. Then he turned to Susan.

'Are you sure your money's all there?'

She fumbled in her purse and nodded, thanking him.

'Are you sure?' The landlord turned to Jake. 'And are you sure you're blind, lad? It seems to me you can see more than the rest of us.'

Jake flushed with pleasure and smiled, hearing Susan saying he was the best brother in the world, a remark he would like to be able to frame and hang up on her bedroom wall, to remind her.

When they had retrieved Susan's bag from the litter bin in the car-park and thanked the landlord once again, they walked to the corner of the road. And stopped. The crossing here was a difficult one, even for people who could see. A man had been knocked down only the other week. There was a filter arrow and no beep-beep-beep to tell you when it was safe to cross. Jake could feel Susan fidgeting beside him. He knew her hand was itching to take his arm but she was afraid of offending him.

'It's all right, Sue,' he said, taking pity on her. 'You go off and get your bus. Dolly will see me across the road, won't you, Doll? I know I can't do this one on my own. Don't want to get squashed, do I?'

'Come on, then, you old bat,' Dolly said, and he felt her warm hand take his, and one of her brothers, Dave or Pete, he didn't know which, clutch his other arm with sticky fingers. 'Come on, me darling.'

Crossing the road with Dolly and her brothers, Jake began to whistle cheerfully a line from a popular song,

'I get by with a little help from my friends.'

'Gone To Sea'

MICHAEL MORPURGO

William Tregerthen had the look of a child who carried all the pain of the world on his hunched shoulders. But he had not always been like this. He is remembered by his mother as the happy, chortling child of his infancy, content to bask in his mother's warmth and secure in the knowledge that the world was made just for him. But with the ability to walk came the slow understanding that he walked differently from others and that this was to set him apart from everyone he loved. He found he could not run with his brothers through the high hay fields, chasing after rabbits; that he could not clamber with them down the rocks to the sea but had to wait at the top of the cliffs and watch them hop-scotching over the boulders and leaping in and out of the rock pools below.

He was the youngest of four brothers born onto a farm that hung precariously along the rugged cliffs below the Eagle's Nest. The few small square fields that made up the farm were spread, like a green patchwork, between the granite farmhouse and the grey-grim sea, merging into gorse and bracken as they neared the cliff top. For a whole child it was a paradise of adventure and mystery, for the land was riddled with deserted tin miners' cottages and empty, ivy-clad chapels that had once been filled with boisterous hymns and sonorous prayer. There were deserted wheel houses that loomed out of the mist, and dark, dank caves that must surely have been used by wreckers and smugglers. Perhaps they still were.

But William was not a whole child; his left foot was turned inwards and twisted. He shuffled along behind his older brothers in a desperate attempt to stay with them and to be part of their world. His brothers were not hard-souled children, but were merely wrapped in their own fantasies. They were pirates and smugglers and revenue men, and the shadowing presence of William was beginning already to encroach on their freedom of movement. As he grew older he was left further and further behind and they began to forget about him or to treat him as if he were not there. Finally, when William was just about school age, they rejected him outright for the first time. 'Go home to Mother,' they said. 'She'll look after you.'

William did not cry, for by now it came as no shock to him. He had already been accustomed to the aside remarks, the accusing fingers in the village and the assiduously averted eyes. Even his own father, with whom he had romped and gambolled as an infant, was becoming estranged and would leave him behind more and more when he went out on the farm. There were fewer rides on the tractor these days, fewer invitations to ride up in front of him on his great shining horse. William knew that he had become a nuisance. What he could not know was that an inevitable

guilt had soured his father who found he could no longer even look on his son's stumbling gait without a shudder of shame. He was not a cruel man by nature, but he did not want to have to be reminded continually of his own inadequacy as a father and as a man.

Only his mother stood by him and William loved her for it. With her he could forget his hideous foot that would never straighten and that caused him to lurch whenever he moved. They talked of the countries over the sea's end, beyond where the sky fell like a curtain on the horizon. From her he learned about the wild birds and the flowers. Together they would lie hidden in bracken watching the foxes at play and counting the seals as they bobbed up and down at sea. It was rare enough for his mother to leave her kitchen but whenever she could she would take William out through the fields and clamber up onto a granite rock that rose from the soil below like an iceberg. From here they could look up to Zennor Quoit above them and across the fields towards the sea. Here she would tell him all the stories of Zennor. Sitting beside her, his knees drawn up under his chin, he would bury himself in the mysteries of this wild place. He heard of mermaids, of witches, of legends as old as the rock itself and just as enduring. The bond between mother and son grew strong during these years; she would be there by his side wherever he went. She became the sole prop of William's life, his last link with happiness; and for his mother her last little son kept her soul singing in the midst of an endless drudgery.

For William Tregerthen, school was a nightmare of misery. Within his first week he was dubbed 'Limping Billy'. His brothers, who might have afforded some protection, avoided him and left him to the mercy of the mob. William did not hate his tormentors any more than he hated wasps in September; he just wished they would go away. But they did not. 'Limping Billy' was a source of infinite amusement that few could resist. Even the children William felt might have been friends to him were seduced into collaboration. Whenever they were tired of football or of tag or skipping, there was always 'Limping Billy' sitting by himself on the playground wall under the fuchsia hedge. William would see them coming and screw up his courage, turning on his thin smile of resignation that he hoped might soften their hearts. He continued to smile through the taunting and the teasing, through the limping competitions that they forced him to judge. He would nod appreciatively at their attempts to mimic the Hunchback of Notre Dame, and conceal his dread, and his humiliation when they invited him to do better. He trained himself to laugh with them back at himself; it was his way of riding the punches.

His teachers were worse, cloaking their revulsion under a veneer of pity. To begin with they over-burdened him with a false sweetness and paid him far too much loving attention; and then because he found the words difficult to spell and his handwriting was uneven and awkward, they began to assume, as many do, that one unnatural limb somehow infects the whole and turns a cripple into an idiot. Very soon he was dismissed by his teachers as unteachable and ignored thereafter.

It did not help either that William was singularly unchildlike in his appearance. He had none of the cherubic innocence of a child; there was no charm about him, no redeeming feature. He was small for his age; but his face carried already the mark of years. His eyes were dark and deep-set, his features pinched and sallow. He walked with a stoop, dragging his foot behind him like a leaden weight. The world had taken him and shrivelled him up already. He looked permanently gaunt and hungry as he sat staring out of the classroom window at the heaving sea beyond the fields. A recluse was being born.

On his way back from school that last summer, William tried to avoid the road as much as possible. Meetings always became confrontations, and there was never anyone who wanted to walk home with him. He himself wanted less and less to be with people. Once into the fields and out of sight of the road he would break into a staggering, ugly run, swinging out his twisted foot, straining to throw it forward as far as it would go. He would time himself across the field that ran down from the road to the hay barn, and then throw himself at last face down and exhausted into the sweet warmth of new hay. He had done this for a few days already and, according to his counting, his time was improving with each run. But as he lay there now panting in the hay he heard someone clapping high up in the haystack behind him. He sat up quickly and looked around. It was a face he knew, as familiar to him as the rocks in the fields around the farm, an old face full of deeply etched crevasses and raised veins, unshaven and red with drink. Everyone around the village knew Sam, or 'Sam the Soak' as he was called, but no one knew much about him. He lived alone in a cottage in the churchtown up behind the Tinners' Arms, cycling every day into St Ives where he kept a small fishing boat and a few lobster pots. He was a fair-weather fisherman, with a ramshackle boat that only went to sea when the weather was set fair.

Whenever there were no fish or no lobsters to be found, or when the weather was blowing up, he would stay on shore and drink. It was rumoured there had been some great tragedy in his life before he came to live at Zennor, but he never spoke of it so no one knew for certain.

'A fine run, Billy,' said Sam; his drooping eyes smiled gently. There was no sarcasm in his voice but rather a kind sincerity that William warmed to instantly.

'Better'n yesterday anyway,' William said.

'You should swim, dear lad,' Sam sat up and shook the hay out of his hair. He clambered down the haystack towards William, talking as he came. 'If I had a foot like that, dear lad, I'd swim. You'd be fine in the water, swim like the seals I shouldn't wonder.' He smiled awkwardly and ruffled William's hair. 'Got a lot to do. Hope you didn't mind my sleeping awhile in your hay. Your father makes good hay, I've always said that. Well, I can't stand here chatting with you, got a lot to do. And, by the by dear lad, I shouldn't like you to think that I was drunk.' He looked hard down at William and tweaked his ear. 'You're too young to know but there's worse things can happen to a man than a twisted foot, Billy, dear lad. I drink enough, but it's just enough and no more. Now you do as I say, go swimming. Once in the water you'll be the equal of anyone.'

'But I can't swim,' said William. 'My brothers can but I never learnt to. It's difficult for me to get down on the rocks.'

'Dear lad,' said Sam, brushing off his coat. 'If you can run with a foot like that, then you can most certainly swim. Mark my words, dear lad; I may look like an old soak—I know what they call me—but drink in moderation inspires great wisdom. Do as I say, get down to the sea and swim.'

William went down to the sea in secret that afternoon because he knew his mother would worry. Worse than that, she might try to stop him from going if she thought it was dangerous. She was busy in the kitchen so he said simply that he would make his own way across the fields to their rock and watch the kestrel they had seen the day before floating on the warm air high above the bracken. He had been to the seashore before of course, but always accompanied by his mother who had helped him down the cliff path to the beach below.

Swimming in the sea was forbidden. It was a family edict, and one observed by all the farming families around, whose respect and fear of the sea had been inculcated into them for generations. 'The sea is for fish,' his father had warned them often enough. 'Swim in the rock pools all you want, but don't go swimming in the sea.'

With his brothers and his father making hay in the high field by the chapel William knew there was little enough chance of his being discovered. He did indeed pause for a rest on the rock to look skywards for the kestrel, and this somehow eased his conscience. Certainly there was a great deal he

73

had not told his mother, but he had never deliberately deceived her before this. He felt however such a strong compulsion to follow Sam's advice that he soon left the rock behind him and made for the cliff path. He was now further from home than he had ever been on his own before.

The cliff path was tortuous, difficult enough for anyone to negotiate with two good feet, but William managed well enough using a stick as a crutch to help him over the streams that tumbled down fern-green gorges to the sea below. At times he had to go down on all fours to be sure he would not slip. As he clambered up along the path to the first headland, he turned and looked back along the coast towards Zennor Head, breathing in the wind from the sea. A sudden wild feeling of exuberance and elation came over him so that he felt somehow liberated and at one with the world. He cupped his hands to his mouth and shouted to a tanker that was cruising motionless far out to sea:

'I'm Limping Billy Tregerthen,' he bellowed, 'and I'm going to swim. I'm going to swim in the sea. I can see you but you can't see me. Look out fish, here I come. Look out seals, here I come. I'm Limping Billy Tregerthen and I'm going to swim.'

So William came at last to Trevail Cliffs where the rocks step out into the sea but even at low tide never so far as to join the island. The island where the seals come lies some way off the shore, a black bastion against the sea, warning it that it must not come any further. Cormorants and shags perched on the island like sinister sentries and below them William saw the seals basking in the sun on the rocks. The path down to the beach was treacherous and William knew it. For the first time he had to manage on his own, so he sat down and bumped his way down the track to the beach.

He went first to the place his brothers had learnt to swim, a great green bowl of sea water left behind in the rocks by the tide. As he clambered laboriously over the limpet-covered rocks towards the pool, he remembered how he had sat alone high on the cliff top above and watched his brothers and his father diving and splashing in the pool below, and how his heart had filled with envy and longing. 'You sit there, with your mother,' his father had said. 'It's too dangerous for you out there on those rocks. Too dangerous.'

'And here I am,' said William aloud as he stepped gingerly forward onto the next rock, reaching for a hand-hold to support himself. 'Here I am, leaping from rock to rock like a goat. If only they could see me now.'

He hauled himself up over the last lip of rock and there at last was the pool down below him, with the sea lapping in gently at one end. Here for the first time William began to be frightened. Until this moment he had not fully understood the step he was about to take. It was as if he had woken suddenly from a dream: the meeting with Sam in the hay-barn, his triumphant walk along the cliff path, and the long rock climb to the pool. But now as he looked around him he saw he was surrounded entirely by sea and stranded on the rocks a great distance out from the beach. He began to doubt if he could ever get back; and had it not been for the seal William would most certainly have turned and gone back home.

The seal surfaced silently into the pool from nowhere. William crouched down slowly so as not to alarm him and watched. He had never been this close to a seal. He had seen them often enough lying out on the rocks on the island like great grey cucumbers and had spotted their shining heads floating out at sea. But now he was so close he could see that the seal was looking directly at him out of sad, soulful eyes. He had never noticed before that seals had whiskers. William watched for a while and then spoke. It seemed rude not to.

'You're in my pool,' he said. 'I don't mind really, though I was going to have a swim. Tell you the truth, I was having second thoughts anyway, about the swimming I mean. It's all right for you, you're born to it. I mean you don't find getting around on land that easy, do you? Well nor do I. And that's why Sam told me to go and learn to swim, said I'd swim like a seal one day. But I'm a bit frightened, see. I don't know if I can, not with my foot.'

The seal had vanished as he was speaking, so William lowered himself carefully step by step down towards the edge of the pool. The water was clear to the bottom, but there was no sign of the seal. William found it reassuring to be able to see the bottom, a great slab of rock that fell away towards the opening to the sea. He could see now why his brothers had come here to learn, for one end of the pool was shallow enough to paddle whilst the other was so deep that the bottom was scarcely visible.

William undressed quickly and stepped into the pool, feeling for the rocks below with his toes. He drew back at the first touch because the water stung him with cold, but soon he had both feet in the water. He looked down to be sure of his footing, watching his feet move forward slowly out into the pool until he was waist-high. The cold had taken the breath from his body and he was tempted to turn around at once and get out. But he steeled himself, raised his hands above his head, sucked in his breath and inched his way forward. His feet seemed suddenly strange to him, apart from him almost and he wriggled his toes to be sure that they were still attached to him. It was then that he noticed that they had changed. They had turned white, dead white; and as William gazed down he saw that his left foot was no longer twisted. For the first time in his life his feet stood parallel. He was about to bend down to try to touch his feet, for he knew his eyes must surely be deceiving him, when the seal reappeared only a few feet away in the middle of the pool. This time the seal gazed at him only for a few brief moments and then began a series of water acrobatics that soon had William laughing and clapping with joy. He would dive, roll and twist, disappear for a few seconds and then materialise somewhere else. He circled William, turning over on his back and rolling, powering his way to the end of the pool before flopping over on his front and aiming straight for William like a torpedo, just under the surface. It was a display of comic elegance, of easy power. But to William it was more than this, it became an invitation he found he could not refuse.

The seal had settled again in the centre of the pool, his great wide eyes beckoning. William never even waited for the water to stop churning but launched himself out into the water. He sank of course, but he had not expected not to. He kicked out with his legs and flailed his arms wildly in a supreme effort to regain the surface. He had sense enough to keep his mouth closed but his eyes were wide open and he saw through the green that the seal was swimming alongside him, close enough to touch. William knew that he was not drowning, that the seal would not let him drown; and with that confidence his arms and legs began to move more easily through the water. A few rhythmic strokes up towards the light and he found the air his lungs had been craving for. But the seal was nowhere to be seen. William struck out across to the rocks on the far side of the pool quite confident that the seal was still close by. Swimming came to William that day as it does to a dog. He found in that one afternoon the confidence to master the water. The seal however never reappeared, but William swam on now by himself until the water chilled his bones, seeking everywhere for the seal and calling for him. He thought of venturing out into the open ocean but thought better of it when he saw the swell outside the pool. He vowed he would come again, every day until he found his seal.

William lay on the rocks above the pool, his eyes closed against the glare of the evening sun off the water, his heart still beating fast from the exertion of his swim. He lay like this, turning from time to time until he was dry all over. Occasionally he would laugh out loud in joyous celebration of the first triumph of his life. Out on the seal island the cormorants and shags were startled and lifted off the rocks to make for the fishing grounds out to sea, and the colony of seals was gathering as it always did each evening.

As William made his way along the cliff path and up across the fields towards home he could hear behind him the soft hooting sound of the seals as they welcomed each new arrival on the rocks. His foot was indeed still twisted, but he walked erect now, the stoop had gone from his shoulders and there was now a new lightness in his step.

He broke the news to his family at supper that evening, dropped it like a bomb and it had just the effect he had expected and hoped for. They stopped eating and there was a long heavy silence whilst they looked at each other in stunned amazement.

'What did you say, Billy?' said his father sternly, putting down his knife and fork.

'I've been swimming with a seal,' William said, 'and I learnt to swim just like Sam said. I climbed down to the rocks and I swam in the pool with the seal. I know we mustn't swim in the sea but the pool's all right isn't it?'

'By yourself, Billy?' said his mother, who had turned quite pale. 'You shouldn't have, you know, not by yourself. I could have gone with you.'

'It was all right, Mother,' William smiled up at her. 'The seal looked after me. I couldn't have drowned, not with him there.'

Up to that point it had all been predictable, but then his brothers began to laugh, spluttering about what a good tale it was and how they had actually believed him for a moment; and when William insisted that he could swim now, and that the seal had helped him, his father lost his patience. 'It's bad enough your going off on your own without telling your mother, but then you come back with a fantastic story like that and expect me to believe it. I'm not stupid, lad. I know you can't climb over those rocks with a foot like that; and as for swimming and seals, well it's a nice story, but a story's a story, so let's hear no more of it.'

'But he was only exaggerating, dear,' said William's mother. 'He didn't mean . . .'

'I know what he meant,' said his father. 'And it's your fault, like as not, telling him all these wild stories and putting strange ideas in his head.'

William looked at his mother in total disbelief, numbed by the realisation that she too doubted him. She smiled sympathetically at him and came over to stroke his head.

'He's just exaggerating a bit, aren't you, Billy?' she said gently.

But William pulled away from her embrace, hurt by her lack of faith.

'I don't care if you don't believe me,' he said, his eyes filling with tears. 'I know what happened. I can swim I tell you, and one day I'll swim away from here and never come back. I hate you, I hate you all.'

His defiance was punished immediately. He was sent up to his room and as he passed his father's chair he was cuffed roundly on the ear for good measure. That evening, as he lay on his bed in his pyjamas listening to the remorseless ker-thump, ker-thump of the haybaler outside in the fields, William made up his mind to leave home.

His mother came up with some cocoa later on as she always did, but he pretended to be asleep, even when she leant over and kissed him gently on the forehead.

'Don't be unhappy, Billy,' she said. 'I believe you, I really do.'

He was tempted at that moment to wake and to call the whole plan off, but resentment was still burning too strongly inside him. When it mattered she had not believed him, and even now he knew she was merely trying to console him. There could be no going back. He lay still and tried to contain the tears inside his eyes.

Every afternoon after school that week William went back down to the beach to swim. One of his brothers must have said something for word had gone round at school that 'Limping Billy' claimed that he had been swimming with the seals. He endured the barbed ridicule more patiently than ever because he knew that it would soon be over and he would never again have to face their quips and jibes, their crooked smiles.

The sea was the haven he longed for each day. The family were far too busy making hay to notice where he was and he was never to speak of it again to any of them. To start with he kept to the green pool in the rocks. Every afternoon his seal would be there waiting for him and the lesson would begin. He learnt to roll in the water like a seal and to dive deep exploring the bottom of the pool for over a minute before surfacing for air. The seal teased him in the water, enticing him to chase, allowing William to come just so close before whisking away out of reach again. He learnt to lie on the water to rest as if he were on a bed, confident that his body would always float, that the water would always hold it up. Each day brought him new technique and new power in his legs and arms. Gradually the seal would let him come closer until one afternoon just before he left the pool William reached out slowly and stroked the seal on his side. It was a gesture of love and thanks. The seal made no immediate attempt to move away but turned slowly in the water and let out a curious groan of acceptance before diving away out of the pool and into the open sea. As he watched him swim away, William was sure at last of his place in the world.

With the sea still calm next day William left the sanctuary of the pool and swam out into the swell

of the ocean with the seal alongside him. There to welcome them as they neared the island were the bobbing heads of the entire seal colony. When they swam too fast for him it seemed the easiest, most natural thing in the world to throw his arms around the seal and hold on, riding him over the waves out towards the island. Once there he lay out on the rocks with them and was minutely inspected by each member of the colony. They came one by one and lay beside him, eyeing him wistfully before lumbering off to make room for the next. Each of them was different and he found he could tell at once the old from the young and the female from the male. Later, sitting cross-legged on the rocks and surrounded entirely by the

83

inquisitive seals, William tasted raw fish for the first time, pulling away the flesh with his teeth as if he had been doing it all his life. He began to murmur seal noises in an attempt to thank them for their gift and they responded with great hoots of excitement and affection. By the time he was escorted back to the safety of the shore he could no longer doubt that he was one of them.

The notepad he left behind on his bed the next afternoon read simply: 'Gone to sea, where I belong.' His mother found it that evening when she came in from the fields at dusk. The Coastguard and the villagers were alerted and the search began. They searched the cliffs and the sea shore from Zennor Head to Wicca Pool and beyond, but in vain. An air-sea rescue helicopter flew low over the coast until the darkness drove it away. But the family returned to the search at first light and it was William's father who found the bundle of clothes hidden in the rocks below Trevail Cliffs. The pain was deep enough already, so he decided to tell no one of his discovery, but buried them himself in a corner of the cornfield below the chapel. He wept as he did so, as much out of remorse as for his son's lost life.

Some weeks later they held a memorial service in the Church, attended by everyone in the village except Sam whom no one had seen since William's disappearance. The Parochial Church Council was inspired to offer a space on the Church wall for a memorial tablet for William, and they offered to finance it themselves. It should be left to the family they said, to word it as they wished.

Months later Sam was hauling in his nets off Wicca Pool. The fishing had been poor and he expected his nets to be empty once again. But as he began hauling it was clear he had struck it rich and his heart rose in anticipation of a full catch at last. It took all his strength to pull the net up through the water. His arms ached as he strained to find the reserves he would need to haul it in. He had stopped hauling for a moment to regain his strength, his feet braced on the deck against the pitch and toss of the boat, when he heard a voice behind him.

'Sam,' it said, quietly.

He turned instantly, a chill of fear creeping up his spine. It was William Tregerthen, his head and shoulders showing above the gunwale of the boat.

'Billy?' said Sam. 'Billy Tregerthen? Is it you, dear lad? Are you real, Billy? Is it really you?' William smiled at him to reassure him. 'I've not had a drink since the day you died, Billy, honest I haven't. Told myself I never would again, not after what I did to you.' He screwed up his eyes. 'No,' he said. 'I must be dreaming. You're dead and drowned. I know you are.'

'I'm not dead and I'm not drowned, Sam,' William said. 'I'm living with the seals where I belong. You were right, Sam, right all along. I can swim like a seal, and I live like a seal. You can't limp in the water, Sam.'

'Are you really alive, dear lad?' said Sam. 'After all this time? You weren't drowned like they said?'

'I'm alive, Sam, and I want you to let your nets down,' William said. 'There's one of my seals caught up in it and there's no fish there I promise you. Let them down, Sam, please, before you hurt him.'

Sam let the nets go gently hand over hand until the weight was gone.

'Thank you, Sam,' said William. 'You're a kind man, the only kind man I've ever known. Will you do something for me?' Sam nodded, quite unable to speak any more. 'Will you tell my mother that I'm happy and well, that all her stories were true, and that she must never be sad. Tell her all is well with me. Promise?'

'Course,' Sam whispered. 'Course I will, dear lad.'

And then as suddenly as he had appeared, William was gone. Sam called out to him again and again. He wanted confirmation, he wanted to be sure his eyes had not been deceiving him. But the sea around him was empty and he never saw him again.

William's mother was feeding the hens as she did every morning after the men had left the house. She saw Sam coming down the lane towards the house and turned away. It would be more sympathy and she had had enough of that since William died. But Sam called after her and she had to turn to face him. They spoke together for only a few minutes, Sam with his hands on her shoulders, before they parted leaving her alone again with her hens clucking impatiently around her feet. If Sam had turned as he walked away he would have seen that she was smiling through her tears.

The inscription on the tablet in the Church reads:

WILLIAM TREGERTHEN

AGED 10

Gone to sea, where he belongs

The Mega-Nuisance

GERALDINE KAYE

'Paddy, you should shut your mouth when you're eating,' Rosalind said crossly. 'I don't want to see all your chewed up liver and bacon, thanks very much.'

'You know he finds it difficult, Rozzy,' Mum said gently. 'Especially now with this awful cold and his nose stuffed up, poor little chap.'

Rosalind said nothing. A seven-year-old brother like Paddy who was all hugs and kisses, who needed it? she thought.

'Your audition tomorrow, isn't it?' Daddy said as if her bad mood needed explaining. 'Don't let it get to you, poppet. It's not the end of the world if you don't get in.'

'I know,' Rosalind said out loud but secretly she thought it *would* be the end of the world. She had been thinking about the audition, working towards it, ever since she had done her first ballet exam and Miss Reid had put her into the acceler ation class for gifted pupils. In October she had got through the preliminary audition for entrance to White Lodge, the Royal Ballet School at Richmond. Now it was February and tomorrow was the *final* audition. They lived too far away for daily travel. She would have to board and the best thing about that was she would only have to put

up with Paddy at half-term and holidays. If she got
into White Lodge.

'Wozzy?' Paddy said, smiling widely as Mum
wiped his face and hands and let him get down
from his chair. He couldn't say his 'r's properly.
'Wozzy?' He was beside her now, pulling at her
skirt and staring up at her with his eyes like grey
marbles. 'Wozzy wead . . . ? Wozzy wead . . . ?'

'Sorry,' Rosalind said getting up. She kicked off
her shoes and gripped the back of her chair and
raised one leg to illustrate. 'I'm busy, Paddy. I've
got to do a *barre* tonight.' She had to see to her
pointes and her ribbons and practise her *pliés* but
you couldn't explain things like that to Paddy.

89

Miss Reid had said her *pliés* could let down her whole *enchaînement*. Even the greatest dancers had stronger and weaker parts to their dancing, Miss Reid said.

'Wozzy wead . . . ? Wozzy wead . . . ?' Paddy said batting the book against her.

'Oh, read to him for a minute while we wash up, there's a love,' Mum said. 'You're his favourite person, you know.'

'Big deal,' Rosalind said. He certainly wasn't hers and she couldn't pretend. She wasn't good at pretending.

'Wozzy wead . . . ?'

'Oh, all right, mega-nuisance,' Rosalind said walking off to the sitting-room. 'Bring your book then.'

How could you be fond of somebody you don't like looking at, she wondered as he scrambled on to her lap and put his arms lovingly round her neck. A long time ago, alone in the sitting-room with Paddy, she had held his lips closed between her fingers as if she could change him. Perhaps Paddy had wanted her to change him too because he hadn't pulled away. He just stared at her with tears running down his face.

He had been four then. She had been four when he was born. 'Why is he so ugly?' she had said, seeing him at the hospital for the first time. She was too young to know it was better not to say things like that. 'Poor little chap, poor little boy,' Mum had said, rocking him tenderly. Had she ever held her like that when she was a baby, Rosalind wondered.

Afterwards, Daddy had explained that Paddy was a Down's syndrome child, some people called it mongol. He would always have some trouble learning to do things, but he should be able to go to school and learn to read and write. Later he might get a job doing simple work. He was delicate too: he had cold after cold. His heart was damaged and his lungs didn't work properly. They would all have to work hard helping Paddy to learn to keep his tongue in and his mouth closed. Daddy said there were many things Paddy would do very well, but he might take a long time to learn.

Rosalind tried hard to be nice to Paddy like Mum was. But it was just too difficult. How could she bring friends home, for instance, with him in the house. Once she had heard girls in the cloak-room whispering, 'Have you seen her brother? Well, he's funny.'

'He's not funny,' she had shouted, erupting through the thicket of coats like an avenging angel. 'He's Down's syndrome, so there.'

They had gone pink and Tracey's mouth fell open like a parody of Paddy's. Well, it would all be different if she got into White Lodge. All her form were going to Hill Street Comprehensive next year and she need never see any of them again. And nobody from White Lodge need ever see Paddy, if she didn't want them to.

'Wead us . . . wead us . . .' Paddy had opened the book and was snuggling against her. His fair hair still smelled of liver and bacon.

91

His favourite story was *The Tin Soldier* by Hans Andersen and that was odd because it had been her favourite story too. The tin soldier was disabled with only one leg, she supposed, but he stood straight and true whatever happened, even when he was swallowed by a big fish. The tin soldier loved the paper dancer, and no wonder, Rosalind thought, she loved her too. The little dancer who stood on the mantlepiece was partly herself of course. But why did Paddy love the story? He wasn't anything like the tin solider who stood true and steadfast whatever happened, or anybody else in the story unless it was the fish with the big swallowing mouth.

Still it was the story he always wanted read. Not that she really had to read it because she knew it by heart. She recited her way through while Mum and Daddy cleared the table.

'Goodnight, mega-nuisance,' she said as Daddy gave Paddy a piggy-back upstairs to bed. They were both so good with Paddy, made such a fuss of him. Once she had tried to say something about it and Mum had said, 'Well, of course . . . they didn't think he'd survive . . . I mean we're lucky to have him . . . we have to make the most of him while . . . because . . .' She never finished the sentence, just blinked and added, 'Oh, sorry, Rozzy dear . . .' But it was clear what she meant.

That evening Rosalind darned the toes of her *pointes* with pink silk more carefully than she had ever done before. Everything was ready for the next day but the night was full of restless, anxious dreams. Saturday morning was sunny, the sky a comforting Cambridge blue as Rosalind got dressed. Mum was going to drive her to Richmond.

'Car?' said Paddy running to the door after breakfast. 'Me come in car?'

'You're not taking him?' Rosalind said.

'Well, he does love the car so,' Mum said apologetically. 'Daddy's going to take him to Richmond Park to see the deer while you're having your audition.'

'No,' said Rosalind. Somebody might see him and nobody from White Lodge was ever going to see Paddy. 'I'm not going then.' She sat down in the chair in the hall. 'If you're taking Paddy, I'm not going.'

There was a pause. Daddy and Mum looked at each other and then Daddy said. 'Tell you what, we'll go to the park here, Paddy, eh? Feed the ducks.'

'Park with Wozzy . . . ?' Paddy said looking from one face to the other uncertainly.

'Better get going, you two,' Daddy said crisply. 'Good luck, poppet, I'm sure you'll do fine.'

'Thanks,' said Rosalind. They set off. It was a two hour journey and Mum didn't say a word, but her lips pressed together said a silent *selfish*. And Rosalind couldn't get Paddy's disappointed face out of her head which was really unfair, she thought, because she *ought* to be thinking about her *pliés* which Miss Reid said was the one thing which might let her down.

She never really knew what happened. All she

heard was a screech of brakes and then a stupendous crash and a jerk which flung her against her seat belt, then the side of the Mini caved in like toffee. A shower of glass and then blackness.

She woke up in hospital. Daddy was there and her leg was hurting badly and so was her head.

'What happened? Where's Mum?'

'Don't worry, love. She's quite all right. She's at home with Paddy. Nothing but a few bruises. It was you who copped it, you've broken your leg.'

'What . . . ?' It was dark outside. 'What time is it?'

'About seven o'clock.'

'The audition . . . ?'

'I'm afraid it was all over long ago,' Daddy said.

'Did I . . . didn't I . . . ?' She still didn't know what had happened. She didn't know anything except there was this awful pain in her leg. And thousands of bandages.

'The car was hit by a lorry,' Daddy explained taking her hand. 'You've been concussed. Your leg was badly broken. They had to put a pin in it, bit of metal or plastic or something. But the doctor thinks you'll be quite all right eventually. Probably not even a limp.'

'Eventually?' Rosalind whispered. How long was eventually.

She stared at the pale grey walls of the women's surgical ward. Everybody said she was very brave. At first the woman in the next bed tried to talk but Rosalind turned away. For a bit she wondered if she could have an audition later, next year say, they took people at twelve, didn't they. But then Miss Reid came to see her and she shook her head. 'Such a shame, this setback,' she said, but a lifetime of teaching ballet had accustomed her to setbacks. She smiled at Rosalind kindly. 'I daresay you'll be able to go on with your grades later on,' she said vaguely. She didn't come again.

Daddy or Mum came every day. They brought books and puzzles and things to do but Rosalind took no interest. She had no interest in anything. Going to White Lodge had been the first step to a ballet career and if she couldn't take even the first step, she didn't want to take any step at all.

'You're not dying, you know,' the physiotherapist said quite irritably one day. 'You really must try to work at your exercises or you won't improve.'

'I don't care,' Rosalind said. She couldn't pretend. She had never been good at pretending.

One afternoon Tracey and Holly came from Grove Road Primary. The top class had drawn getwell cards. Nearly all of them had a ballet girl standing on her *pointes*.

'Thanks,' Rosalind said and her eyes filled with tears.

'I don't suppose you'll be going to that school, will you, that posh ballet school? I mean it's great, you'll be coming to Hill Street Comprehensive with the rest of us, eh?' Tracey said, trying to be nice. Rosalind just stared at them with tears streaming down her face until a nurse led them away. 'It's no good being sorry for ourselves,' the same nurse said later that evening. 'You're lucky to be alive, young lady.' Rosalind had stopped crying then. She put the ballet girl cards under her pillow.

'How's Paddy?' she said when Mum came that evening.

'He's all right. Well, he's got a bit of a cold as a matter of fact and a chesty cough. Doctor's put him on antibiotics and he's got to stay in bed. Still he's a good little patient. He talks about you all the time. He'd got Granny reading him *The Tin Soldier* when I left. Nothing ever seems to get him down . . . so brave . . . marvellous really.'

'Mm,' said Rosalind. At first she was glad not to be there, listening to Paddy coughing in the next room. But that night she woke and looked at the moon shining pale through the curtains and she wondered if he was all right.

'Why don't you bring Paddy to see me?' she said that next day. She was sitting in a chair by this time.

'Well . . . we didn't think you . . .'

'I'd really *like* to see him,' she said. 'I mean it's been ages.'

'Well, when he's better . . . He's still got a temperature, you know.' Mum looked worried when she spoke but Rosalind didn't realize how worried until after she had gone. That night she woke and lying in the ward with quiet breathing all round her, she was sure that something awful was happening to Paddy. And the more she thought about it the more she was sure that he was really

sick. Paddy who loved her most in the world was really ill and she might never see him again and they weren't telling her . . . just making excuses . . .

'Where's Paddy?' she said quite loudly when Daddy came next day and several heads turned to look. 'Why didn't you bring him?'

'Paddy? He's all right,' Daddy said. 'He's outside as a matter of fact. Mum thought they'd better wait in the car. Well, his temperature's down but he's still got a bit of a cold.'

'I want to see him,' Rosalind almost shouted.

'Well, okay, poppet,' Daddy said. 'No need to get all het up.' He waved from the window, beckoning.

She could see at once that Paddy was all right when he came running into the ward.

'Wozzy . . . Wozzy . . . Wozzy,' he shouted, scrambling joyfully on to the bed and hugging her, anointing her cheek with two weeks' supply of wet kisses. He was just the same, grey eyes, blond hair. 'Wozzy wead . . . Wozzy wead book.'

'Oh, all right, mega-nuisance,' she said and Paddy grinned hugely at the familiar word. The book fell open at the right page and she began to recite. The woman in the next bed was smiling, whispering to Mum, 'Ever so good with him, isn't she?'

She was like the paper dancer, Rosalind thought, listening to the sound of her own voice, the paper dancer who had been burned up in the fire. That was right. But Paddy wasn't like the big-mouthed fish at all. He was like the tin soldier who stood brave and true on his one leg and went on loving the paper dancer whatever happened.

Paddy *was* the tin soldier, steadfast to the end.

I Can Jump Puddles

ALAN MARSHALL

Alan Marshall contracted poliomyelitis shortly after starting school. It left him without the use of his legs, but more determined than ever to prove he could do things just as well as his friends. In this extract Alan has been teaching himself to ride, without telling his parents.

I continued taking Starlight to the trough but now I never cantered him till he was on the track to the school and the turn-off to the lane was behind him.

I had often tried to ride with only one hand clinging to the pommel of the saddle, but the curvature of my spine made me lean to the left and one hand on the pommel did not prevent a tendency for me to fall in that direction.

One day, while Starlight was walking, I began gripping the saddle in various places, searching for a more secure position on which to hold. My left hand, owing to my lean in that direction, could reach far lower than my right while I was still relaxed. I moved my seat a little to the right in the saddle then thrust my left hand under the saddle

flap beneath my leg. Here I could grasp the surcingle just where it entered the flap after crossing
the saddle. I could bear down upon the inner
saddle pad to counter a sway to the right or pull on
the surcingle to counter a sway to the left.

For the first time I felt completely safe. I crossed
the reins, gripping them with my right hand,
clutched the surcingle and urged Starlight into a
canter. His swinging stride never moved me in the
saddle. I sat relaxed and balanced, rising and
falling with the movement of his body and exper-
iencing a feeling of security and confidence I had
not known before.

Now I could guide him. With a twist of my hand
I could turn him to the right or the left and as he
turned I could lean with him and swing back again
as he straightened to an even stride. My grip on
the surcingle braced me to the saddle, a brace that
could immediately adjust itself to a demand for a
steadying push or pull.

I cantered Starlight for a little while then, on a
sudden impulse, I yelled him into greater speed. I
felt his body flatten as he moved from a canter into
a gallop. The undulating swing gave way to a
smooth run and the quick tattoo of his pounding
hooves came up to me like music.

It was too magnificent an experience to repeat,
to waste in a day. I walked him back to the school
humming a song. I did not wait for Bob to leg me
off; I slid off on my own and fell over on the
ground. I crawled to my crutches against the wall
then stood up and led Starlight to the pony yard.

When I unsaddled him and let him go I stood leaning on the fence just watching him till the bell rang.

I did not concentrate on my lessons that afternoon. I kept thinking about father and how pleased he would be when I could prove to him I could ride. I wanted to ride Starlight down next day and show him, but I knew the questions he would ask me, and I felt that I could not truthfully say I could ride until I could mount and dismount without help.

I would soon learn to get off, I reflected. If I got off beside my crutches I could cling to the saddle with one hand till I got hold of them and put them

101

beneath my arms. But getting on was another matter. Strong legs were needed to rise from the ground with one foot in the stirrup. I would have to think of another way.

Sometimes when romping at home I would place one hand on top of our gate and one on the armpit rest of a crutch, then raise myself slowly till I was high above the gate. It was a feat of strength I often practised, and I decided to try it with Starlight in place of the gate. If he stood I could do it.

I tried it next day but Starlight kept moving and I fell several times. I got Joe to hold him, then placed one hand on the pommel and the other on the top of the two crutches standing together. I drew a breath, then swung myself up and on to the saddle with one heave. I slung the crutches on my right arm, deciding to carry them but they frightened Starlight and I had to hand them to Joe.

Each day Joe held Starlight while I mounted but in a fortnight the pony became so used to me swinging on to the saddle in this fashion that he made no attempt to move till I was seated. I never asked Joe to hold him after that, but I still could not carry my crutches.

I showed Bob how I wanted to carry them, slung on my right arm, and asked him would he ride Starlight round while he carried my crutches in this fashion. He did it each afternoon after school was out and Starlight lost his fear of them. After that he let me carry them.

When cantering they clacked against his side

and at a gallop they swung out, pointing backwards, but he was never afraid of them again.

Starlight was not tough in the mouth and I could easily control him with one hand on the reins. I rode with a short rein so that, by leaning back, I added the weight of my body to the strength of my arm. He responded to a twist of the hand when I wished him to turn and I soon began wheeling him like a stockpony. By thrusting against the saddle pad with the hand that held the surcingle I found I could rise to the trot, and my bumping days were over.

Starlight never shied. He kept a straight course and because of this I felt secure and was not afraid of being thrown. I did not realise that normal legs were needed to sit a sudden shy since I had never experienced one. I was confident that only a bucking horse could throw me and I began riding more recklessly than the boys at school.

I galloped over rough ground, meeting the challenge it presented to my crutches by spurning it with legs as strong as steel — Starlight's legs which now I felt were my own.

Where other boys avoided a mound or bank on their ponies, I went over them, yet when walking it was I who turned away and they who climbed them.

Now their experiences could be mine and I spent the school dinner hour in seeking out places in which I would have found difficulty in walking, so that in riding through or over them, I became the equal of my mates.

Yet I did not know that such was my reason. I rode in these places because it pleased me. That was my explanation.

Sometimes I galloped Starlight up the lane. The corner at the end was sharp and turned on to a metal road. The Presbyterian Church was built on the opposite corner and it was known as the 'Church Corner'.

One day I came round this corner at a hard gallop. It was beginning to rain and I wanted to reach the school before I got wet. A woman walking along the pathway in front of the church suddenly put up her umbrella and Starlight swerved away from it in a sudden bound.

I felt myself falling and I tried to will my bad leg to pull the foot from the stirrup. I had a horror of being dragged. Father had seen a man dragged with his foot caught in the stirrup and I could never forget his description of the galloping horse and the bouncing body.

When I hit the metal and knew I was free of the saddle I only felt relief. I lay there a moment wondering whether any bones were broken then sat up and felt my legs and arms which were painful from bruises. A lump was rising on my head and I had a gravel rash on my elbow.

Starlight had galloped back to the school and I knew that Bob and Joe would soon be along with my crutches. I sat there dusting my trousers when I noticed the woman who had opened the umbrella. She was running towards me with such an expression of alarm and concern upon her face that I looked quickly round to see if something terrible had occurred behind me, something of which I was not aware. But I was alone.

'Oh!' she cried. 'Oh! You fell! I saw you. You poor boy! Are you hurt? Oh, I'll never forget it!'

I recognised her as Mrs Conlon whom mother knew and I thought, 'She'll tell Mum I fell. I'll have to show Dad I can ride tomorrow.'

Mrs Conlon hurriedly placed her parcels on the ground and put her hand on my shoulder, peering at me with her mouth slightly open.

'Are you hurt, Alan? Tell me. What will your poor mother say? Say something.'

'I'm all right, Mrs Conlon,' I assured her. 'I'm waiting for my crutches. Joe Carmichael will bring my crutches when he sees the pony.'

I had faith in Joe attending to things like that. Bob would come running down full of excitement, announcing an accident to the world; Joe would be running silently with my crutches, his mind busy on how to keep it quiet.

'You should never ride ponies, Alan,' Mrs Conlon went on while she dusted my shoulders. 'It'll be the death of you, see if it isn't.' Her voice took on a tender, kindly note and she knelt beside me and bent her head till her face was close to mine. She smiled gently at me. 'You're different from other boys. You never want to forget that. You can't do what they do. If your poor father and mother knew you were riding ponies it would break their hearts. Promise me you won't ride again. Come on, now.'

105

I saw with wonder that there were tears in her eyes and I wanted to comfort her, to tell her I was sorry for her. I wanted to give her a present, something that would make her smile and bring her happiness. I saw so much of this sadness in grown-ups who talked to me. No matter what I said I could not share my happiness with them. They clung to their sorrow. I could never see a reason for it.

Bob and Joe came running up and Joe was carrying my crutches. Mrs Conlon sighed and rose to her feet, looking at me with tragic eyes as Joe helped me up and thrust my crutches beneath my arms.

'What happened?' he demanded anxiously.

'He shied and tossed me,' I said, 'I'm all right.'

'Now we'll all shut up about this,' whispered Joe looking sideways at Mrs Conlon. 'Keep it under your hat or they'll never let you on a horse again.'

I said goodbye to Mrs Conlon who reminded me, 'Don't forget what I told you, Alan,' before she went away.

'There's one thing,' said Joe, looking me up and down as we set off for the school. 'There's no damage done; you're walking just as good as ever.'

Next day I rode Starlight home during lunch hour. I did not hurry. I wanted to enjoy my picture of Father seeing me ride. I thought it might worry Mother but Father would place his hand on my shoulder and look at me and say, 'I knew you could do it,' or something like that.

He was bending over a saddle lying on the ground near the chaff house door when I rode up to the gate. He did not see me. I stopped at the gate and watched him for a moment then called out, 'Hi!'

He did not straighten himself but turned his head and looked back towards the gate behind him. For a moment he held this position while I looked, smiling, at him, then he quietly stood erect and gazed at me for a moment.

'You, Alan!' he said, his tone restrained as if I were riding a horse a voice could frighten into bolting.

'Yes,' I called. 'Come and see me. You watch. Remember when you said I'd never ride? Now, you

watch. Yahoo!' I gave the yell he sometimes gave when on a spirited horse and leant forward in the saddle with a quick lift and a sharp clap of my good heel on Starlight's side.

The white pony sprang forward with short, eager bounds, gathering himself until, balanced, he flattened into a run. I could see his knee below his shoulder flash out and back like a piston, feel the drive of him and the reach of his shoulders to every stride.

I followed our fence to the wattle clump then reefed him back and round, leaning with him as he propped and turned in a panel's length. Stones scattered as he finished the turn; his head rose and fell as he doubled himself to regain speed: then I was racing back again while Father ran desperately towards the gate.

I passed him, my hand on the reins moving forward and back to the pull of Starlight's extended head. Round again and back to a skidding halt with Starlight's chest against the gate. He drew back dancing, tossing his head, his ribs pumping. The sound of his breath through his distended nostrils, the creak of the saddle, the jingle of the bit were the sounds I had longed to hear while sitting on the back of a prancing horse and now I was hearing them and smelling the sweat from a completed gallop.

I looked down at Father, noticing with sudden concern that he was pale. Mother had come out of the house and was hurrying towards us.

'What's wrong, Dad?' I asked, quickly.

'Nothing,' he said. He kept looking at the ground and I could hear him breathing.

'You shouldn't have run like that to the gate,' I said. 'You winded yourself.'

He looked at me and smiled, then turned to mother who reached out her hand to him as she came up to the gate.

'I saw it,' she said.

They looked into each other's eyes a moment.

'He's you all over again,' Mother said, then turning to me, 'You learned to ride yourself, Alan, did you?'

'Yes,' I said, leaning on Starlight's neck so that my head was closer to theirs. 'For years I've been learning. I've only had one buster; that was yesterday. Did you see me turn, Dad?' I turned to Father. 'Did you see me bring him round like a stockhorse? What do you think? Do you reckon I can ride?'

'Yes,' he said. 'You're good; you've got good hands and you sit him well. How do you hold on? Show me.'

I explained my grip on the surcingle, told him how I used to take Starlight to drink and how I could mount or dismount with the aid of my crutches.

'I've left my crutches at school or I'd show you, I said.

'It's all right . . . Another day . . . You feel safe on his back?'

'Safe as a bank.'

'Your back doesn't hurt you, does it, Alan?'

Mother asked.

'No, not a bit,' I said.

'You'll always be very careful, won't you, Alan? I like seeing you riding but I wouldn't like to see you fall.'

'I'll be very careful,' I promised, then added, 'I must go back to school; I'll be late.'

'Listen, son,' Father said, looking up at me with a serious face. 'We know you can ride now. You went past that gate like a bat out of hell. But you don't want to ride like that. If you do people will think you're a mug rider. They'll think you don't understand a horse. A good rider hasn't got to be rip-snorting about like a pup off the chain just to show he can ride. A good rider don't have to prove nothing. He studies his mount. You do that. Take it quietly. You can ride – all right, but don't be a show-off with it. A gallop's all right on a straight track but the way you're riding, you'll tear the guts out of a horse in no time. A horse is like a man; he's at his best when he gets a fair deal. Now, walk Starlight back to school and give him a rub down before you let him go.'

He paused, thinking for a moment, then added, 'You're a good bloke, Alan. I like you and I reckon you're a good rider.'

The New Girl at Blane

MABEL ESTHER ALLAN

'Who's the new kid?'

'I dunno. She's old to be new. Old as we are. She'll be in the top class.'

'Shall we go and speak to her?'

'No, don't let's. She doesn't look very friendly.'

It wasn't that I wasn't friendly. I was just trying to get my bearings in the new world of town and a far bigger school than the one I had left. I'd have had to leave, anyway, even if we hadn't come to live in Southwich. Everyone had to leave at eleven, but Blane Road Middle School kept boys and girls for another year.

There was nothing wrong with my ears, even though the playground was filling with a noisy, moving crowd. I was standing in the morning shadow near the main entrance, but the rest of the scene was bathed in brilliant early September light. It helped me in a way, but it would be difficult when we went into school, for the corridors were dark in places. No unexpected steps, though. I had been with my mother the day before, to see the headmaster.

I blinked into the glare, seeing figures slightly blurred, and the scene beyond was blurred, too, but I could see a nearby factory, bright red, and a blue truck passing on the road.

The group that was talking about me was a little apart from the noisy crowd. Suddenly they moved nearer and I saw that there were two girls and two boys. One of the boys was black.

'I'm going to speak to her,' the black boy said. 'Horrible being new.' He was the one with the nicest voice, and he seemed to have a nice face, too. So had the fair girl who advanced with him. The other two hesitated, giggling.

'She looks like an owl!' the other boy said, quite loudly, and I could have killed him, even though I should have been used to my ugly thick glasses after wearing similar ones since I was about three.

If I'd gone to a special school, as some people had suggested, would anyone have been so unkind? Or bad-mannered? They were used to me at the village school, and didn't make personal remarks.

'Hello! I'm Justin Carlow.' The black boy was smiling. 'An' this is Liz Whitting. The other two are Suzanne and Phil. What's your name?'

'Ginny Brown,' I answered. If I'd said Ginevra Gabrielle Brown they'd have laughed, however polite they were. My mother was in a romantic mood when I was born. Too bad she got a daughter with smooth, mouse-brown hair and grey-green eyes that weren't much use.

'Why've you come to Blane now?'

I started to explain that my father had had an accident and couldn't do his old job, so we had come to live near his brother, my Uncle Charlie. I had just got to: 'He's almost able to walk properly now, and Uncle Charlie is giving him a job in his shop . . .' when the bell rang and we went in to Assembly in the big hall.

I stuck to Justin and Liz to make sure I was going to the right place and the right seats, though the other girl, who had red hair, said: 'She'll be in B. She looks dopey.'

'I'm in A,' I cried. 'Mr Bagshaw said so.'

Mrs Jones at my old school gave me a good report. I wasn't very good at figures, but anything that needed imagination, like history and English, was easy to me. I liked geography, too. Bad sight soon gives you an excellent memory.

The light in the hall was very tiresome, striking across from large windows. The platform was a distant blur, but I knew by the sudden silence when the teachers came in. We oldest ones were sitting at the back.

Mr Bagshaw wasn't a Cheshire man; he came from Lancashire. He had a broad, deep voice and rather a hearty manner. But I had liked him well enough. He hadn't seemed to pity me.

'Ginny'll manage,' he had said to my mother. 'I'll explain to the staff.'

I'd manage if it killed me. But during the hymn (I hated hymns, for even the cheerful ones made me miserable) a wave of depression went over me. I didn't want to live in Southwich, and I knew my parents disliked it, too. Poor Dad wasn't cut out to work in a shop, though Uncle Charlie had been very good.

Southwich was an old 'salt' town, with several

ancient half-timbered buildings, but our street was ugly, and there was no green anywhere. The houses were right on the pavement.

Mr Bagshaw made a short speech and then began to give out lists and notices. He reminded us that one of the special features of Blane Road was our school outings. Different classes would be going to Chester Zoo and Manchester Airport.

'But the first trip is already arranged for the two top classes,' he explained. 'In less than a fortnight ... now aren't you lucky? You're going to Welladine Manor and the ruins of Welladine Castle. The Manor is a lovely old half-timbered house. Part of it is fifteenth century, and there are two secret rooms.'

I hardly heard the applause and murmuring around me. I must have jumped, for Justin turned to look at me. I stared straight ahead. I was hot all over and the sweat was pouring down my nose under my heavy glasses.

A few minutes later we were entering what seemed to be a big, cheerful classroom. The teacher, standing just inside the door, stopped me as I went past. 'You're Ginny Brown, aren't you?' she asked. 'I'm Mrs Clark. You're to sit at the front.'

'Oh, Mrs Clark, can't Ginny sit at the back with Liz and me?' Justin cried.

That was very friendly of him, but it was no good. Part of my problem was that I always had to sit near the front, and even then I couldn't really see the board.

When she marked the register Mrs Clark called me 'Ginevra Gabrielle Brown', which caused a titter. I still felt rather sick after the shock I had had in the hall, but I managed to say:

'Please, I'm *always* Ginny.'

'All right, Ginny,' Mrs Clark answered, very nicely. 'But not on the register. Everyone has to be grand on that.'

Until break we were given copies of our timetable and lists of text books and exercise books we had to get from the stockroom. The timetable was so palely printed that I had to read with my nose almost on it, but I managed everything all right.

Out in the playground I stood aside, thinking of that school outing. The others were all rushing about, throwing balls or having mock fights. Suddenly Suzanne yelled: 'Catch, Ginny!' I put up my hand defensively, but the ball hit me on the shoulder.

'Butter-fingers!' Suzanne cried, as she dived for the ball.

'I don't think she can see,' said Justin's voice.

'She ought to be able to with those great thick glasses!'

I definitely hated Suzanne, but I liked Justin.

'Can't you see?' asked Liz, at my elbow.

'Not very well. Some things, but not fast balls. The light makes a difference.'

It wasn't a good day. I used my ears and my nose, and my eyes as much as I could, and I began to get some faces and voices sorted out. I didn't eat much dinner, though it was quite good, and I hid

in the girls' toilets until school started again. Justin and Liz were quite friendly when I gave them the chance, though a bit awkward, but the others seemed to avoid me, and whispered about me.

'Where d'you live, Ginny?' Liz asked, at the end of school, and I told her Victoria Street. It seemed that she and Justin lived the other way, and I was glad. It was better out, alone. The sun was hot on my head as I walked through the narrow streets.

'How did it go, Ginny?' my mother asked anxiously.

'Not so bad,' I told her. 'I managed. There's a nice boy called Justin. He's black. I never met a black boy before. There seem to be quite a lot . . . girls,

116

too.' I wondered whether to tell her about the outing, but decided against it. I wouldn't go to Welladine Manor, anyway.

For homework we had to write a piece about Tudor England, which we'd had a lesson about that afternoon. It could be an essay, a story or even a poem. They had all groaned, but that was something I could do well. I got out my lovely new exercise book, thought for a few minutes, then began to write. It was a story about what happened to a young monk when King Henry the Eighth's men came to plunder his abbey. I was happy doing that.

Next morning I handed in *Escape from the Abbey* with confidence. That was Wednesday, and not much better than my first day, though I managed most of the work pretty well. Somehow I couldn't be friendly, and I thought most of the others despised me, or thought me rather strange. I didn't want to be strange, different. I wanted to be ordinary.

'But do you really?' I asked myself. I wanted to see ordinarily, but I meant, one day, to be Ginevra G. Brown, the famous novelist. What'd they say if I told them that?

On Friday afternoon Mrs Clark read out some of the essays and pieces we had written. Mine didn't come, and I felt hot. But it was last. Mrs Clark said: 'Your English is excellent, Ginny.' She read out *Escape from the Abbey,* and even Suzanne listened without giggling and pushing her neighbour.

117

It was my first triumph, but I felt it didn't make them like me any better. I didn't blame them, really. I would have *liked* to be friendly, if only the spell that held me would break. Out of class I had lost the use of my tongue. I didn't even find it when I heard Phil say: 'Bet she copied it from somewhere.'

On the way home I made myself see all I could. I looked at every crack in a wall, at every weed, and at the black and white patterns of the old buildings. At the same time I wished violently that I was back in the country.

I could have the country by going on the school outing, but one day wouldn't be enough, and . . . well, I *couldn't* go.

But then it turned out that everyone was going, and there was surprise and consternation when I began to say I wasn't going.

Mrs Clark said: 'I should have thought, Ginny dear . . .' and, to stop her, I said: 'Oh, all right.' After all, it was probably just a kind of cowardice.

So I told my mother we were going into the country on Monday and she gave me the money without asking any questions. She was preoccupied. Trying, like me, to get used to changes.

Justin made an effort on Friday afternoon. He really was nice. 'Sit with us in the bus on Monday, Ginny. We'll tell you things. It must be horrible not to see.'

'Thanks,' I answered, but when Monday came, and the two buses were at the gates, I slid into a little single seat by the driver. Everyone bumped past me, laden with bags containing their picnic food and bottles of lemonade. We were to eat by the River Dee.

Mrs Clark wasn't with us, and I was glad. She might have said something tactless. She had twisted her ankle on Saturday. The two teachers with us were unknown to me. It was a relief.

In spite of myself I felt a surge of excitement as we headed across the flat Cheshire countryside. I could see golden stubble fields, and cottage gardens filled with a blur of purple and gold. Michaelmas daisies and golden rod? I hardly heard the shouting and singing. I was alone in my skin, half-seeing, but I felt better than for a long time.

It was only about fifteen miles, but oh! the difference. After the hot bus the air was sweet and mellow, and there were hills not far away. There was a picnic site by the river, and a place for parking. But there was nobody else there. The river flowed softly, for it was deep in that part, and there was an old red sandstone bridge.

One of the teachers, Mr Tagg, yelled to everyone to shut up. Suzanne and Phil were the last to be quiet and settle down at one of the tables provided. They were quite clever in their way, but by then I knew they were regarded as school nuisances, often in trouble.

'Now get this clear, the lot of you,' said Mr Tagg. 'Anyone who falls into the river, misbehaves at the Manor, or breaks their necks at the castle will be left in the country.' He said it as if it was a fate worse than death, and everyone laughed,

119

apparently agreeing. Except Justin, who whispered to me: 'I shouldn't mind.'

I nodded. I definitely liked him, if only my silly tongue would loosen up and let me be friendly.

'The village of Welladine is over the bridge,' Mr Tagg went on. 'And the castle ruins are quite near. The Dee isn't the boundary between England and Wales at this point. The Manor is this side. Now don't take forever putting away all that food.'

I ate the delicious sandwiches my mother had made for me, and drank the warmish lemonade, but the feeling of the place was much more important. The trees showed no trace of autumn, and I knew there were wild flowers everywhere. I longed to be alone and not with fifty-nine others, and four teachers.

After the picnic the two classes split up. One party set off over the bridge to the castle, and we started off up the narrow lane to the Manor. I walked in the rear, or tried to. Once Suzanne bumped into me, sort of accidentally on purpose, then ran on. I heard her say: 'If anyone breaks her neck it'll be Ginny!'

It wouldn't, then. But I had other thoughts and feelings, and didn't mind much just then, for we soon came to the Tudor gatehouse. A woman was waiting with tickets, and I looked at her curiously. She was middle-aged and rather plump, and she hadn't a local voice. She looked bored.

'My husband is expecting you,' she said. 'Go straight on and into the courtyard.'

Soon I saw the Manor, asleep in its green hollow.

The house had a sandstone base, and the rest was intricate black and white timbering. Gables, old twisted chimneys, windows with small, leaded panes.

Everyone had gone quiet, for Mr Tagg had added another threat. Anyone who was a nuisance could go and sit in the bus, and he was the one who would wait with them.

The house made a square around the cobble-stone courtyard, and we entered the courtyard by way of a shadowy passage under the Long Gallery. One of the other teachers, Miss Barlow, had bought a guide book and paused to read some of it to us.

Then the custodian appeared and took over, and we all trooped into the oldest part and stood in the kitchen, with its huge inglenook fireplace, ancient cooking implements and shining copper pots and pans.

'Of course,' explained the custodian, who said his name was Thwaite, 'we have a modern kitchen in our living quarters.' And he made some rather flat jokes about cooking in past times.

The banqueting hall went up to the roof, with a gallery, and there were Michaelmas daisies and dahlias on a great oak table. I breathed deeply of the smell of polish and oldness. I was lost in dreams and hardly heard what was said.

I followed everywhere. Once Liz stopped and asked: 'Are you all right, Ginny?' For some of the passages were very dark, and there were unexpected twisting stairs. But I walked surely. I

121

watched the opening of a secret door in the panelling, and, as a few at a time were allowed into the hidden room, I moved away to the window.

Outside the light was golden-bright, and I could see the hills, or perhaps I knew they were there, beyond a gap in the trees.

There was one place in the fifteenth century wing, where the way was blocked by a thick rope and a notice saying: 'Danger. Keep out.' Mr Thwaite explained that some parts weren't safe. The Trust for Ancient Houses had allocated some money, and work would soon begin on restoration.

He sounded bored. He didn't describe the house and its quiet history with much vividness. No wonder some of us were growing noisy and restless again. But most of them showed interest when we were led back to the banqueting hall, where there was a sales table in a corner displaying postcards and other small things.

It was then that I slipped away, up a side staircase and back to the Long Gallery. The roof was of ancient oak beams, and, though the floor was uneven now, people had danced there in past centuries. Light fell on the polished floor in dazzling patterns from the diamond panes of the little windows. I blinked to get used to the change after the dark staircase, and suddenly I was happy.

I took a few dancing steps, and then I heard quick feet on the stairs and swung around. Justin's voice cried in surprise:

'Ginny! They haven't missed *you*. Tagg sent me

to look for Suzanne and Phil, and Liz came, too. He's furious!'

The spell was broken. I said: 'I haven't seen them.'

Not far from the foot of the stairs was the danger notice, and suddenly my sharp ears heard a giggle and then a splutter, both very familiar. Suzanne had clapped her hand over her mouth.

Then, almost at once, there was a piercing scream, followed by a cracking, splitting sound.

I scrambled over the rope and Justin and Liz came after me.

'Be careful, Ginny!' Justin cried anxiously. 'We'd better tell . . .'

'Wait!' I ordered. My voice came out authoritative and loud. I went along the narrow passage to the light beyond. It dazzled me for a few moments, then I saw into the room. It was a large room, once a drawing room, quite unfurnished. Suzanne was over near the window. I saw the sun on her red hair and white face. The centre of the floor had broken and Phil was half-way down the hole, his hands clutching the jagged edges, his mouth open to yell. He was facing our way. Instead of yelling, he gasped:

'I'm going down into the cellars. I'll be killed! Help! Someone get hold of me!'

I heard Justin say: 'Go an' tell 'em, Liz!' But I was already going forward cautiously.

'Stop panicking, Phil,' I ordered. 'You won't go down at all if you *listen*. There'll be a beam somewhere under your feet. Find it!'

123

Phil gasped and writhed, and Suzanne began to cry. But after a moment Phil said: 'I've got it! It's quite firm, I *think*.'

'It will be,' I said, hoping I was right and it wasn't rotten. Then I ordered Suzanne to work her way around the wall, away from the cracks spreading over the floor. And I told Justin to do as I did. I lay down on my front and wriggled forward. I took one of Phil's hands, after a few moments when he refused to let go. His fingers were cold with strain, and he clutched wildly. Justin, lying beside me, took the other. He'd kept his head, unlike Suzanne, who was still crying loudly. Over her sobs I heard approaching footsteps, but there was no time to lose.

'Now fish with one foot,' I said. 'There'll be a bit of beam higher, with luck. That's it. Now heave.'

And, just as people arrived in the doorway behind us, up Phil came. I am pretty strong. It's only my eyes that are weak. I knew I was getting badly scratched by the sharp edges of the hole and Phil gave a shriek of agony. But, as Justin heaved, too, he sprawled almost on top of us.

'Well, I'll be darned!' cried Mr Tagg's voice. But he said no more until we had all crawled to safety, and by then most of our class seemed to be crowding in the passage behind him. Mr Thwaite was there, too, and very angry.

'Blessed kids! Might have been killed. Me and the wife are sick of this place already. Give me a modern house every time. You all deserve to be whipped.'

'Not Ginny!' gasped Phil. 'She saved my life. Suzanne and me were exploring an' the rotten floor went. An' Ginny came . . .'

'Justin helped,' I said calmly. 'And you wouldn't have gone into the cellar. The land rises this side of the house. There's only a low passage under here, leading to a side door.'

Everyone had gone quite silent. I had cut my hand and wrist and they were bleeding. Sunlight and shadows were making it hard to see.

'I'll be *darned!*' Mr Tagg said again. 'Ginny Brown, aren't you? The girl who doesn't see well. So how'd you . . . ?'

I felt tired, but calm. 'I don't need to see here. I've lived here since I was two. My dad was custodian until he had an accident. I know every inch of this house. I miss it all the time.'

After Mr Thwaite had found disinfectant and plaster, and Miss Barlow had dealt with our wounds, we all went back into the courtyard. Phil looked the worst. He had awful scratches, and his shirt was torn and bloody. As I went out last Mr Thwaite said to me: 'I'd heard about your dad. We only came here because I'd lost my job in Manchester. How's your dad now?'

'Better,' I told him. 'And hating living in Southwich.'

'Well, we won't be staying here beyond next summer. May be joining our son in Canada. Tell your dad to get in touch with the Trust.'

My heart was light as I walked down the lane with Justin and Liz, and Suzanne and Phil were near by, not giggling and being silly.

'*Wasn't* there a cellar under there?' asked Phil.

'No, there wasn't,' I said cheerfully. 'But you might have broken your leg. And it would have served you right.'

'Why didn't you tell us you lived there?' Justin asked.

'I don't know. I didn't want to talk about it. It was so awful coming away to Southwich.' Then I made a great effort and went on: 'Look, I'm sorry I wasn't friendly. I was miserable, that's all. But now . . .'

I had found my tongue, I had done something that had impressed them, and probably I could bear Southwich for a few months, until next summer. Welladine would still be there, waiting. It had been there for hundreds of years already. A few months would not make much difference to that house in a green hollow close to the River Dee.

The Tinker's Curse

JOAN AIKEN

One winter evening an old tinker who travelled from village to village selling his wares came to an isolated farmhouse which stood on the shore of a wide water. There were no other buildings near, and no sound to be heard but the distant cries of sheep, grazing on the moors.

But a light shone in the window of the little house, which cheered the tinker, who was hungry, and weary from his day's wandering.

He unpacked and set out his tray of goods, played a few notes on his bagpipes, and sang his tinker's chant:

> *Buy my beads and bobbins*
> *My laces, silks and ribbons*
> *Threads and pins and buttons*
> *None so good as mine!*

Then he knocked hopefully at the door. Usually, in such a lonely spot, he might be sure of a seat by the fire, a drink and a good meal, and an evening spent in singing songs and telling all the news of the country he had passed through.

How could he know that the house belonged to a heartless and wicked couple, a robber and his wife, who, without the least scruple, knocked the tinker on the head, cut his throat, and stole his money and goods. His body they tied to a stone and sank

'I'll fetch a doctor, sweetheart, never fear,' said John, and he dropped his hammer and raced off towards the nearest village, three miles away down at the foot of the loch.

But while he was on his way, dusk fell, and the tinker's ghost came up out of the water, playing a wild and grieving tune on his pipes. And the ghost sang:

> *If any hear me*
> *Who will not help me*
> *On you I lay my bane*
> *Who will not help me*
> *May ill befall you*
> *Woman, child, or man!*

The young wife heard him, and she shuddered in terror. 'Ghost, ghost, what have I ever done to you that you should hurt me?'

But, taking no notice of her, the spectre sang:

> *If you hear me*
> *And do not help me*
> *If I cry in vain*
> *Hear no sound*
> *From this day forward,*
> *Never hear again!*

When the young husband and the doctor came panting back to the croft, they found that they had come too late. For the wife had given birth to her baby, but now lay dead and cold, killed by the tinker's curse. Only the baby lived, wailing with hunger in her mother's arms.

'Take comfort, at least, from the child,' said the doctor. 'It's a bonny lass – see her sweet face.'

131

But John fell into a rage.

A bonny lass?
My wife is gone?
I want no lass
I want a son!

And from that day on, John retired into a hard shell of anger and useless grief and disappointment. He never spoke to Helen, his little daughter, except to scold or curse her; though she grew up pretty as a wild-rose, and sweet-tempered, worked as hard as she could to please him, and never said a word to provoke him.

How could she? For she was deaf. Doomed by the tinker's curse, she had never heard a single sound since the moment of her birth. She could not hear the lark twitter, nor the lambs bleat; she could not hear the fox bark, nor the curlew call; she could not hear the wind in the rowans, nor the patter of rain on the roof. And (more luckily for her) she could not hear her father's angry voice, though she could see his furious face. She lived in a shell of silence, as he did in a shell of anger.

And, because Helen could hear nothing, she was not able to speak. For how can you learn to use words if you have never heard them?

The children from the village at the loch-foot used to tease Helen. Because she could not speak, they thought she was daft, simple-minded. They used to dance round her, singing:

Deafie, daftie, she can't hear
Creep up behind her and pull her hair
Deaf as an adder, deaf as a post

She was cursed by the tinker's ghost –
Let's see who can get up closest!

But Helen's father became even angrier if he
found them teasing her. Not because he cared
about the teasing, but because they kept her from
her work – sweeping, cooking, tending the garden,
feeding the fowls. He would chase the children
away from his door, hurling stones after them, and
furious words:

'Away wi' ye, scoundrelly weans! Let the useless
girl at least get on with her sweeping.'

Helen used to watch the other children wistfully, longing to be allowed to join in their games
when they played Red Rover, or Grandmother's
Steps. But how could she ask? She had no words to
tell what she wanted.

One thing Helen did have. And that, perhaps,
had grown from the fact that, since she could not
hear what they were saying, she watched other
people so very, very closely. She almost seemed
able to discover what was hidden in their minds,
their memories. She was able to tell, if something
had been lost, where it had been left. And this, to
the other children, seemed mysterious, almost
magical.

'Helen, Helen, I've lost my ribbon!' a girl would
cry, pointing to her tangled locks, making gestures
to convey the tying of a hair-ribbon.

Lost my ribbon, where can it be?
Lost my garter climbing a tree
Lost my skip-rope, lost my ball
Don't know where it can be at all!

Shot my arrow into the air
Fell to earth I don't know where
Lost my knife, I lost my pen
Where will I ever find it again?

And, almost every time one of the children had lost some treasure, Helen would be able to lead them to the place where it lay. So, gradually, because of this, the children began to be more friendly to Helen. And a boy called Andie, who was brighter than the rest, and kinder as well, began to teach Helen how to talk in sign-language; and then, putting his hands on either side of her face, helping her mouth to move, he showed her how to make sounds, how to speak words, and name the objects that were all around her.

I, you, he, she, it
Tree, sun, house, trouser, shirt
Arm, leg, hair, cheek, eye,
Grass, flower, dog, bird, sky!
Now do you begin to puzzle it out?
Now d'you start to see what it's all about?

And Helen would slowly answer, with a tongue that felt clumsy and stiff because for twelve years it had never done anything like this:

Yes – now I begin to see
Sun, house, trouser, tree
Yes, now I think I understand
Arm, leg, cheek, hand . . .

But, although she had now begun to talk a little, in a queer, croaking voice, Helen's father never spoke to her. Nor would she have heard him if he had. For she was still deaf. She could not hear thunder, or cuckoos, or the kettle boil, or the bull bellow.

One day, when Helen was about fourteen, a stranger came to the village. He was not really a stranger: he was the doctor who, all those years ago, had arrived too late to save Helen's mother. That failure had made him so sad that he had left the village and gone away to study medicine in a foreign land so that, in the end, he hoped, he might make up, by saving hundreds of lives, curing hundreds of sick people, for that one life he had not been able to save. Now the doctor was wise and famous, head of a great College of Medicine. He had come to visit his old mother.

When he saw Helen, fetching water from the loch, he asked, 'Tell me, who is that lassie?'

And the children told him, 'Ah, she's the deafie, she's the daftie.'

> *Deafie, daftie, she can't hear*
> *Creep behind her and pull her hair*
> *Deaf as an adder, deaf as a post*
> *She was cursed by the tinker's ghost.*

But Andie exclaimed:

> *You are unfair to the girl*
> *She is not daft at all!*
> *She can see further than most*
> *She can find what is lost*
> *Not only lost things can she find*
> *She can read what is in your mind.*

'Talk to her like this, on your hands,' Andie told the doctor. 'She can understand that very well.'

So, talking in sign language on his hands, the

135

doctor asked Helen:

Can you really read my mind?
Do you know what I wish to find?

And Helen answered him directly:

You have lost your watch of gold
That tells both the time and the date
And has your name written inside the case

'How in the world did you know that, lassie?'
exclaimed the doctor.

While you were fishing, up by the loch
The chain was loosened, the watch fell off
Up by the loch you'll find it safe
Under the shade of a foxglove leaf.

Helen led the doctor up to the loch and, sure
enough, there was the watch lying, just where she
had said it would be.

That watch was the gift of a grateful queen
Who was saved by my life-support machine!
I am overjoyed to have it found
I wouldn't have lost it for a thousand pound
What can I give you, Helen my dear?

And she answered:

Help me to hear! Help me to hear!

The doctor looked at her gravely. Then he said,
'Well, take me to your father.'

So she led the doctor to her father's house, and
the doctor said to John: 'I would like to help your
daughter.'

But John burst out, in his usual rage:

The girl's a fool, useless at her work
Deaf as a post, never hears a word
Never hear her laugh, never hear her sing

Never see her smile, never says a thing

> *Fourteen years she has been my blight*
> *Fourteen years next Saturday night*
> *Ever since the curse of the tinker's ghost*
> *When that brat was born and my love was lost.*

'How deaf are you, Helen?' asked the doctor. 'Can you hear this?'

He took a tuning-fork from his bag, knocked it against the stone lintel, to make it hum, and held it, first in front of Helen's ear, then behind the ear, letting it touch the bone. After he had done many other tests, he told Helen and her father:

> *I could help this girl to hear*
> *Two bones have joined inside her ear*
> *With skill, with care*
> *I could give her the power to hear.*

John was not interested.

> *What good can it do?*
> *You might make her worse*
> *She is bound to be deaf*
> *Because of the curse.*

But the boy Andie cried:

> *Please help her, Doctor*
> *With your clever knife*
> *Open up her hearing*
> *To all of life!*

Helen herself wandered outside the cottage to think about what the doctor had said.

> *Do birds really sing?*
> *Do boys really shout?*
> *They open their mouths*

But no sound comes out.

Do dogs really bark
Does the wind really blow?
Does the fire really crackle?
I don't know . . .

What is the sound
Of the sea on the shore
Does the bull bellow
Does the old man snore?

How can I tell
What is being said?
I have had to listen
To thoughts instead.
Then the doctor, coming out, warned her:
Attend now, Helen
Pay good heed
If I try this
It may not succeed.

Or, if you learn to hear
Then you may find
You have lost the power
To read my mind

You may lose the power
To find what's lost—
But Helen cried out:
Doctor, please do it
Whatever the cost!
And the children, gathering round, exclaimed:
What a surprise she's in for

When she first hears thunder
And won't she get a shock
When she first hears Rock!

Oh, but what a pleasure she has in store
To hear her first curlew, bubbling on the shore
– Yeah, but will she think it quite such fun
When she first hears somebody fire a gun?

The doctor took Helen away from the village to a grand hospital, far off in the city. And before he performed the operation on her ears, he warned her:

Helen, this is important
Please pay attention
After the operation
You must lie without moving a muscle
You must lie, still as a mummy
For a twenty-four-hour period
Your head flat, still on the pillow
No jerk, no twitch, no fidget.
Do you understand me?

'Yes,' said Helen. 'I understand.'

I must lie, without moving a muscle
For a twenty-four-hour period.

So Helen was put to sleep, and the doctor, with his tiny, delicate instruments, with wonderful skill and care, undid the two bones that were locked together inside her ear. And then she was wheeled back to her hospital bed, from the theatre where he had done the operation, and then she had to lie, still as a stone, for twenty-four hours. Not a muscle did she move. Her heart beat, her breath

139

went in and out; that was all.

At the end of twenty-four hours, the doctor said to her,

'Helen, can you hear my voice?'

And she answered slowly, 'I am not sure.'

'I am going to put my gold watch beside your ear. Tell me if you can hear it tick.'

Helen listened, with her ear against the watch. She drew in a long, deep breath. Then she whispered:

> *Yes! It goes tick-tick-tick!*
> *Tick – tick – tick – tick*
> *Doctor, I never knew*
> *What a wonderful sound a watch can make*
> *Ticking the whole day through!*
>
> *Tick, tick, tick, tick*
> *Oh, what a beautiful sound*
> *I could lie and listen for ever, for ever*
> *Watching the hands go round!*

When Helen went home to the village, the children came out to meet her, and cried,

> *Helen, can you hear?*
> *Helen, can you hear us?*
> *Did he open up your ears?*
> *Can you hear our chorus?*

And Helen told them:

> *Yes! I can hear, I can truly hear*
> *All of a sudden, the whole world is near*
> *I can hear the trees rustle, hear the birds sing*
> *I can hear the cuckoo, and the church bells*
>   *ring*

I hear the cricket chirping, and the plane
  overhead
I can hear the breadknife, cutting through the
  bread . . .
And they asked her,
Now your ears are open to sound
Can you hear our thoughts go round?
Do you still have that power of the other kind?
Can you still listen to another person's mind?
She told them:
No, I can hear your thoughts no longer
All I can hear is your speaking voice.
But this way round is really better
This way round is the safer choice.

Now I can hear your speaking voices
Nothing is gained without some cost
Now I can hear your thoughts no longer
Nor tell you where are the things you lost.

When he found that she was cured, that she was now like everybody else, Helen's father was sorry indeed that he had been unkind to her for so long. He walked by the loch, and said to himself,
Now her ears are open to sound
I forget my grief that she wasn't a son
I have done her great harm, all through her
  growing
But now I will atone for the wrong that I have
  done.
And he grew so kind that Helen could hardly believe it was the same man who had been sulky and full of rage all through her growing up.

The night that Helen came home, it took her a long time to fall asleep. The sounds of night were so beautiful – the wind, the bleating of sheep, the call of owls, the squeaking of bats – that she lay awake listening. And then, all of a sudden, she heard another sound. It was not her father, for he was down at the village, celebrating with his neighbours.

It was the ghostly tinker, playing a sad wild chant on his ghostly pipes. And he sang:

> *If any hear me*
> *Who will not help me*
> *On you I lay my bane*
> *Who will not help me*

May ill befall you
Woman, child, or man!

Helen, hearing this strange voice, threw a plaid round her shoulders and ran out of the house. And there she saw the tinker's ghost, all dripping wet, in the mist at the water's edge.

She cried:

Who are you, you poor old man?
With your pipes, and your pack?
Why, you are all wet! Let me help you
Take that heavy load from your back!

How can I help you, poor old man
Who have travelled so far?
Will you not come into our house
And sit by our fire?

The ghost told her:

If you would help me, find my poor bones
Where they lie in the dark
Find my skeleton that drifts uneasy
Below the waters of the loch

Bring my bones to the Christian kirkyard
Sort them tidy and bury them there
Wrapped and decent in shroud and coffin
Bid the Minister say a prayer

Set up a stone that tells my story
Only that will give me peace
Only when my bones are buried
Only then can I lie at ease.

And Helen promised:

Yes, I will find them, yes, poor ghost.

> *And bury them safe from wind and weather*
> *Raise a stone that tells the story*
> *Of the poor tinker's brutal murder*
> *Candle and prayer shall help and hush you*
> *Now your curse need travel no further.*

So, the very next day, the tinker's bones were found and raised from the bottom of the loch, and given proper burial. And from that time his ghost haunted the place no longer.

Andie said to Helen, some months later, 'Helen! Do you really not know what I'm thinking any longer? Or can ye not guess?'

And she answered him:

> *People's thoughts should be safe and private*
> *I've lost the power of the other kind —*
> *But tell me what your thought is, Andie*
> *The secret plan you have tucked behind?*

And he said teasingly:

> *By and by I'll be telling you, Helen*
> *Just for the moment — never you mind!*

Mates

ALLAN BAILLIE

The old aluminium dinghy slid back on its dying wave and sat patiently in the mouth of the bay.

'What d'you reckon?' the bigger boy said. He took his hand from the throttle.

The other boy, lean, brown and wearing a camera, was bailing water from the bottom of the dinghy.

'Brian?'

Brian lifted his head. He stood, shaded his eyes and studied the bay. Twin hills, dark with thick bush, dipped to hold the pale beach and the still water in a ragged cup. A few coconut palms thrust from the scrub, but there were no coconuts. From the beach the shallow water stretched almost to the dinghy, but the surface was pricked by a broad pattern of stunted coral.

Brian didn't even open his camera case. 'I dunno, Steve. Not much, is it?'

Steve propped himself on the pillars of his arms. 'Suppose we could go somewhere else.'

'Ah, it's late. The tide's changing.' Brian looked at the southern headland and the distant island, a stone lion in a green sea. 'It'll get better. If you get up high.' Brian tasted his last words and looked at Steve with a quick shrug.

Steve flicked a reassuring smile and pointed at a

rock at the edge of the beach. 'I can fish from there. Like you said, the tide is coming in.'

'Okay, let's get in there.'

Steve turned the throttle a touch and the dinghy nudged into the bay. The dark blue of deep water began to lighten as coral plates and pinnacles slid from the shadows. He slowed the motor to a heart-beat and followed Brian's waving fingers carefully, but the dinghy ran out of water fifty metres from the rock.

Steve killed the motor. 'Sorry,' he said.

'Ah, well . . .' Brian eased himself carefully over-board, placing his sneakers between coral fingers. He carried the anchor to the end of its line and planted it. By the time he returned Steve had bundled his withered legs over the side and was waiting for him with the line, prawn-bait and frying pan.

'You're pretty sure, aincha?' Brian pointed at the pan.

'Got some butter, even. They'll come.'

'Yeah, yeah. Taxi?' Brian backed toward Steve. Steve passed his left arm across Brian's chest, swung his laden right fist clear of the boat and pulled himself onto Brian's back with a heave and a jerk. Brian scooped Steve's legs forward, locked his own hands together and paddled slowly from the dinghy. Half-way to the rock Brian stumbled, took two steps sideways and stopped, leaning on his knees.

'Trouble?' Steve said.

'You're getting fat, that's the trouble.' Brian was

panting.

'There's only half of me.'

'Well, half of you is getting fat.'

Brian took a long breath and paddled on, leaving Steve's limp legs writing a faint trail on the surface of the water. He dumped Brian on the rock and sprang up slightly with the loss of the weight.

'Maybe next time we bring Wheels?' Steve said.

'I should buy a gas balloon. Tow you along.'

'It'll be easy on the way back. Tide'll be in and I can fall in the boat from here.'

'Hey, the tide. How'll you be?'

'The tide mark is way down there. No worries. Go away.'

Brian looked at his camera and a ledge half-way

147

up the slope. 'Okay, see you later.'

'Wait, wait. Get us some wood first, hey?'

'Wood?'

'Maybe you like your fish raw?'

Brian dumped a few armloads on the rock and stepped back. 'That's it. Keep you going till dawn.'

'You be careful up there, okay?'

Brian nodded briefly, then walked across the beach and into the bush.

Steve settled himself on the rock and thought of throwing out the line. He could make the distance – his arms, trained on Wheels, the wheelchair, were as strong as a man's – but the water was too shallow for the fish. Better to watch the tide come in, to flow around the coral stubs and the wet sand shapes, and wait. He could just see the resort where both their parents worked, a dim flash of white in the green of a far island, and if they knew where their kids were now there'd be slaughter in the streets. So what's new?

A flash of white in the darkening green. The fish were coming. Already.

Steve thought a little about Brian as he picked up a prawn and threaded it on the hook.

It was a long time, him and Brian. Him and Brian and Wheels. A lot of parties and movies together. And a few blues, too, like whose turn it is to buy the tickets? He can be a mean fink, sometimes. Still, he's not all that bad, is he? Specially when we leave Wheels behind, like today.

The surface of the bay rippled with small fish leaping low and fast and the water sounded like frying chips.

Steve snorted. He had been drifting toward touchy territory. He never thought about the long friendship he had with Brian, never why nor how. He felt if he prodded it the whole thing would come crashing about his ears. He was around, like the rabbit's foot in his pocket, that was enough.

Something big in the deep water was swirling the surface.

Could Brian see what it was? Steve spotted Brian clawing his way up an almost vertical fall of tangled scrub, like a monkey swinging from branch to root to vine. Steve wrinkled his nose, looked away and looked back.

He's mad. Will take that camera anywhere, any time for a shot. Would spend a week climbing an island mountain just to get a sunset at the end of it. He'd stand on the edge of the crater of an erupting volcano to get the colour of the lava. He's mad . . .

A pattern of fast splashes pulled Steve's eyes down to the sea. Fish were lunging toward him now, closer to the rock. The rock was surrounded by water and the dinghy was drifting past the anchor.

So he climbs mountains. What do you do? Fish.

Steve hurled the hooked prawn against the rushing tide.

Now that's stupid. But they're busy today.

A double handful of white fish exploded from the water and scudded along the surface.

There is something around today.

149

Steve felt his line tug. He jerked hard to set the hook and quickly pulled the white fish to the rock. A garfish. Not big, but tasty. He looked up at the high hill and waved the fish at the silhouette on the rocky ridge.

'Got . . .' he started to shout but realized Brian was looking far above him.

What can he see up there? Wish I could see . . .

Then Steve saw that Brian was looking up into the sky, looking at a circling sea eagle. Probably wishing he could fly . . .

Suddenly Steve was laughing. He rebaited his hook and paid attention to his bay. The water was alive with a rush of garfish now, erupting from the water in scores, squadrons skimming the surface, leaping for the sun. Even the deserted dinghy caught one.

'What is happening?' he said softly.

He threw his hook out and had a garfish on the line almost immediately. He was pulling it in when a great brown shape slid in its flapping wake.

'Get out!' He threw a stone chip at the brown shape as he almost jerked the fish into the air. The turtle surfaced and blinked at him. 'Get your own.' The turtle angled its head, turned and ducked after new prey.

'Oh man, can Brian see this?'

And a pair of dolphins hummed and slid into the bay in slow unison.

Steve stopped fishing. 'Welcome to my banquet,' he said quietly.

And the sea eagle swung down from the empty

sky. It glided easily across the bay, close enough to show its hooked beak, resting claws and its brown and white feathers. A fish hurled itself into the air to escape the turtle and the eagle took it toward the dipping sun without moving a wing.

'Fast food nut,' Steve murmured, and went back to watching the dolphins.

Brian climbed painfully through the last of the scrub, covered in scratches and very tired. He had fallen on the way down, tumbling, skidding toward the edge of a cliff and had been very frightened. Now he stopped on the sand, watching the low glow of the fire and the still shadow on the rock.

He could smell the rich aroma of fresh fish and butter.

Oh, mate, he thought, and closed his eyes. Good ol' Reliable. Master fisherman, top chef, you wouldn't have left me up there with a broken leg. Maybe somehow get into the dinghy and get help, or just keep the fire going until help came. Maybe even swim all the way home. He would. He would do something. Always does.

He walked across the beach to the distant splashes of the water.

'How did it go?' Steve said.

'Wait for the photos,' he said. 'Up there, it was great. There's two beaches, this one and over there one like a mirror, and the island, up there it was gold . . . You just tell me and I'll shut up.'

Steve smiled up at him and pushed the frying pan across. 'It's pretty good down here too,' he said. 'Have a fish.'